KILLING SADIE

KILLING SADIE

RACHEL PETERSON

SIMON PULSE
New York Amsterdam/Antwerp London
Toronto Sydney/Melbourne New Delhi

This book is a work of fiction. Any references to historical events, real people, or real places are used fictitiously. Other names, characters, places, and events are products of the author's imagination, and any resemblance to actual events or places or persons, living or dead, is entirely coincidental.

SIMON PULSE
An imprint of Simon & Schuster Children's Publishing Division
1230 Avenue of the Americas, New York, New York 10020

First Simon Pulse hardcover edition August 2026

Jacket photography by iStock.com

Book design by Heather Palisi
The text of this book was set in Cardo.
Manufactured in China
2 4 6 8 10 9 7 5 3 1
Library of Congress Cataloging-in-Publication Data
Names: Peterson, Rachel, 1989– author
Title: Killing Sadie / Rachel Peterson.
Description: First Simon Pulse hardcover edition. | New York : Simon Pulse, 2026. |
Summary: After Sadie and another teen are murdered at a house party, conflicting stories from her twin, her boyfriend, and her best friend reveal small inconsistencies that add up to big lies.
Identifiers: LCCN 2025037769 (print) | LCCN 2025037770 (ebook) |
ISBN 9798347109869 hardcover | ISBN 9798347109883 ebook
Subjects: CYAC: Murder—Fiction | Twins—Fiction | Sisters—Fiction | Secrets—Fiction | Mystery and detective stories | LCGFT: Detective and mystery fiction | Novels | Fiction
Classification: LCC PZ7.1.P4566 Ki 2026 (print) | LCC PZ7.1.P4566 (ebook)
LC record available at https://lccn.loc.gov/2025037769
LC ebook record available at https://lccn.loc.gov/2025037770

For Ryan and Kristen, whose wise words and perfect timing set this wild ride in motion

KILLING SADIE

LIZ

7:18 A.M., THE MORNING AFTER THE MURDERS

SOUR PATCH KIDS.

That's what I'm thinking about when the police detective walks in the door. He starts talking before it even latches shut behind him. I try to control the feeling of panic that rises up in me when I hear the click that tells me the door is, definitively, shut. It's just him and me—and whoever is probably watching us from behind the two-way mirror.

This is everything my parents always said would end up happening to me. Well, everything my stepfather always said would happen, anyway. Stuck in a police station, trying to explain myself to someone because of something terrible. He just always figured that whatever the terrible thing was, it would be my fault. Everything is my fault to him.

They probably never imagined that the terrible thing would be my best friend's murder. And I swear, I had nothing to do with it. The murder, anyway.

But just because I didn't kill her doesn't mean it isn't my fault.

She's why I'm thinking about Sour Patch Kids. My best friend, Sadie, is, I mean. She always called me "Patch"—a shorthand reference to the fact that there are two pretty extreme sides to my personality. I never minded the nickname. I've been called worse.

"State your name for the record," the detective is saying.

"Liz," I reply without thinking.

"Your full name."

"Elizabeth."

The detective sighs in exasperation and looks at me like he's trying to figure out if I am going to be a total pain in the ass or not. Then he seems to remember my best friend is dead and attempts a smile. It looks more like a grimace. I'm really in no mood for fake sympathy.

"Your full name—first and last."

"Elizabeth Amelia Stratton," I say, my own voice sounding

foreign to my ears. When's the last time I actually had to say my whole name out loud?

When I say it, my Southern drawl comes through. We moved here from Alabama five years ago—that's when I met Sadie, just a few weeks into the school year, when she asked me if my accent was real. I told her it was, and she promised she wouldn't let anybody make fun of me for it. It's a promise she couldn't keep, but I loved her for it, anyway. She also promised she wouldn't tell anyone that I was held back a year when we moved. Pretty sure I'm the only nineteen-year-old senior at our school, but to this day, no one knows. When a friendship starts out like that, with one person sticking up for the other one and keeping her secrets, it never quite evens out. No one tells you that.

At the sound of my voice, the detective visibly softens. They always do. Adults, anyway. Especially men. They look at me, and they see a cute little blond girl with big eyes and a soft Southern twang, and they feel like they should be saving me from something. But there's a really wide gap between adults who *feel* like they should be saving you and adults who actually step in when they see something wrong.

My damsel-in-distress act has its benefits. Mainly, it helped me spend the past three years partying my ass off on the dime of guys who were willing to buy me and my friends a few bottles of vodka from the liquor store. It's not my fault they were stupid enough to think that we'd be drinking it *with* them.

That was the sour side of the Sour Patch Kids joke between me and Sadie. She'd ask if it was going to be a sweet night or a sour one, and whenever I said sour (which was almost always), she knew it meant we were going to get into some trouble and have a damn good time doing it. That's the version of me most kids at school know too. The party girl willing to put it all on the line for a good time. And that's who I was, until it went too far.

I shake my head. Those nights feel like a thousand years ago now. A different girl. A different lifetime. It must have been a different lifetime, because Sadie was with me.

"Thank you. Should I call you Liz, then? Or do you prefer Miss Stratton?" The detective sounds tired as he asks the question and plops down his tragic Styrofoam coffee cup, forcing me back into the present.

It's such a ridiculous question that I don't even bothering answering him. I don't care what he calls me.

I can tell just by the smell coming from his cup that it's more sludge than coffee—the sort you might be able to chew instead of drink. I work part-time as a barista at our local coffee place, and I've become a bit of a coffee snob. Sadie is always teasing me about my new "cosmopolitan tastes." Another inside joke, considering that aside from coffee I still have the taste of a girl who moved to Ohio from a trailer park in Alabama and created a new personality to outrun the old one. Because that's what I am. Sadie still teases me for that too, but in a loving way.

Was always teasing me.

Was. Past tense.

Because the whole reason I'm here, staring down a detective who looks like he stepped directly out of life as an extra on a bad eighties cop show, is because my best friend is dead. She was murdered last night.

Without warning, a wave of nausea hits me.

"I think I might be sick," I say.

The detective grabs a plastic trash can from the corner of the room and hands it to me, and I empty the contents of my stomach.

"Can I have some water, please?" I croak, trying to regain my dignity as I set the can back down. How on earth did I get here, vomiting into a trash can at a police station? It's a rhetorical question, obviously. I know exactly how I got here.

"How much did you drink last night, Miss Stratton?" the detective asks. He's speaking to me with pity in his voice, like he thinks some guy at Trevor McClain's party forced little old me to down a few shots and shotgun a couple of warm beers.

"I don't drink." It's my automatic answer these days.

"Are you sure about that? We're not looking to get anyone in trouble for drinking here. I just need to know how accurate your memories are."

"Yes, I'm sure. I'm not worried about getting in trouble for drinking because I *wasn't* drinking." I really hate that I sound just as deeply annoyed as I am. Probably not a good look at the moment. I try again. "It's true. I used to drink, but I stopped. Maybe six months ago. You can ask anybody; it was kind of a big deal. Everyone thought I was kidding at first. Anyway, I stopped, and that's all there is to it. Now, can I get some water, *please*?"

He gives me a look that suggests this part of the conversation isn't over. I hate when people do that, look at you as if they just *know* they're going to outsmart you. As if they just know you're lying, and nothing you say is going to change that opinion.

"I'll get you water, Miss Stratton. And this doesn't have to be combative. I'm not trying to fight with you; I'm just trying to understand what happened last night. I know you and Sadie Cooper were close—"

"We were best friends."

Even I realize how juvenile it sounds when I say it out loud. But it's true. I instinctively reach for my half of the "Best Friends" necklace Sadie got for us last year. The necklace I literally only take off when I shower. It's been the one constant in my accessories ever since she gave it to me in a cute little purple box on the day after Christmas. I reach for it, but my fingers touch nothing.

Then I remember: The necklace isn't there. It's gone, probably somewhere in the endless fields of the McClain family farm.

Probably gone forever. Just like her.

It's only a necklace, but the loss feels overwhelming. My nausea bubbles back up.

"Right," the detective says, wrenching me away from the horror I'm feeling all over again. "Best friends. And so, since you're her best friend, I'm sure you want answers as much as we do about how she ended up being brutally murdered last night . . ."

"Who else have you talked to?"

I ask the question before I can stop myself. Based on the look the detective gives me, apparently it was the wrong question.

"Why does that matter, Miss Stratton? Is there someone in particular you think we should be talking to?"

"I don't know. Sadie's sister, Jayne? Her boyfriend, Ben? Literally everyone who showed up to Trevor's last night?"

We're interrupted by a uniformed officer, who brings in a bottle of water and sets it down in front of me. For a second, I wonder how she knew I asked for it, but then I remember the two-way mirror. I'm sure the whole thing is being recorded too.

Great.

The detective rubs his eyes. "Look, we got off on the wrong foot here, Miss Stratton. You've been through a lot in the past twelve hours, and I sympathize with that. You must be feeling a million different things right now, and I'm sure you'd rather be anywhere but here. I didn't even introduce myself properly. My name is Detective Norris, and all I care about is understanding what led up to the events of last night."

"And by 'the events,' you mean the fact that my best friend was stabbed to death and then her boyfriend killed the guy who did it." I practically choke on the word "boyfriend." Ben Carrera. God, the look on his face when I walked into that barn. I'll never forget it.

"That is what I mean, yes."

I take a long drink of water, and I realize that my hands are shaking. If Detective Norris notices, he pretends that he doesn't.

"Okay," I say, setting the water back down. "Fine. Where do you want me to start?"

"How about you tell me what happened leading up to the party? Anything you remember that seemed strange or different, anything about Sadie's relationship with"—Detective Norris opens the folder sitting on the table and scans it—"Mason Vreeland?"

I let out a short laugh. I can't help it.

"Something funny about Mason Vreeland, Miss Stratton? Did you know him well?"

"Mason and I were in homeroom together in middle school the year I moved here," I say finally. "He was quiet. Pretty nice, I guess, when he did decide to talk, which wasn't often. But he wasn't bullied or anything like that. Just a loner. If you'd told me that by the time we were in high school, I would be sitting in a police station trying to help the cops understand why he stabbed Sadie to death . . . I don't know. I guess I would have said you were fucking crazy."

"You've got quite a colorful mouth on you, Miss Stratton."

I put my hands up in mock surrender. "I hope I haven't offended your sensibilities, Detective. A lady should certainly watch her language in the middle of a murder investigation."

Classic Liz. I suddenly hear Sadie's voice in my head. She always loved to play armchair psychiatrist. *Lashing out because you don't trust authority.*

Per usual, Sadie's right. She was always right about me.

Detective Norris closes the folder and leans in closer to me from across the table. He's quickly losing his patience with me; I can tell. It's not entirely his fault—I tend to have that effect on people. "Let's just stick with the facts, shall we? Start with yesterday. Tell me everything you remember."

I stare at him, wondering if he's as old as he looks or if it's just the night shift and bad coffee catching up to him. He doesn't look away. Maybe that's the moment I realize there is no getting out of this. No amount of charm or Southern accent or any of the other tricks I've perfected over the years to protect myself will do me any good. Because even if I talk my way out of this room, out of this police station, out of this whole damn town, I'll still be doing it alone. Without Sadie. Without the Cooper family.

So, this detective wants to know about everything that led up to the party. But if he wants to understand Sadie and all the rest of them, it's not just about yesterday or even the past week. It isn't just about the past year.

Sadie is the sister I never had. The only one who actually understood me and somehow loved me and accepted me anyway. Her family is the family mine couldn't be, even if the cracks in their perfect façade started to show in a big way during spring break last year. And I'm the sister Sadie deserved. Sure, she and Jayne were twins. But I was Sadie's best friend. I had the necklace to prove it. Well, I had it first, anyway.

My hand goes up to my neck again, and I remember, again, that my necklace is gone. It feels almost cruel, and I choke back another sob.

"I'm waiting, Miss Stratton." The detective's voice cuts into my thoughts. "Whenever you're ready."

I take a deep breath.

"Okay. Fine. You want to start with what happened yesterday? I'll tell you what happened. But there's gonna be a lot more to it than just the stuff right before the party."

"Well, then, Scarlett O'Hara," he says, clearly delighted by his own joke (and the fact that I'm finally going to play ball with him) and giving me a smile that reminds me of that cat in the Alice in Wonderland books, "enlighten me."

JAYNE

7:18 A.M., THE MORNING AFTER THE MURDERS

"WE'RE GOING TO have to get started with the questions soon, all right?"

The voice sounds like it's far away, or like I have my AirPods in and someone is trying to talk over the music. I shake my head, trying to get my ears right.

"Miss Cooper?" the woman's voice comes again. This time it sounds clearer.

I look up and force myself to focus. There is a uniformed officer sitting across the table from me, and she's the one whose voice I hear. Next to her sits a man who I think introduced himself to me as the lead detective when I first came in here.

Wait, how long have I *been* in here?

"Medical said she's calmed down some, but she may still be in shock," the officer is saying to the detective.

"I respect that, but we need information," he replies. "The more time goes by, the less fresh it's going to be in her mind."

"I can talk," I choke the words out. "And you can call me Jayne." I've been crying for hours. My voice is so hoarse, it doesn't even sound like my own anymore.

Honestly, talking is the last thing I want to do right now. But I know I have to. I have to tell them what happened last night. I was a witness. I held my dying sister in my arms. I need to explain what happened.

It all feels like a dream. But it's not a dream.

This is real.

And I hate to hear them talking about me like I'm not even here, or like I can't understand them.

"Jayne," the detective says, pushing a PowerBar and a cup of what looks like tea toward me across the table. A sad little lemon slice is floating in it. "I'm not sure if you heard me earlier, but I'm Detective Adrian Hunt. I know you've just been through hell, and I'm sorry that you're with us now. I promise, we'll get you out of here and back to your parents as soon as we can. I just need you to tell me anything you know that might help us understand what happened last night."

"'What happened'?" I ask, my voice shaking. "What do you mean, 'what happened'? You know what happened. Mason stabbed my sister, and Ben tried to save her, and Mason went after him, so he had to—" My throat closes up as I try to finish the sentence.

They know what he had to do. They know that Mason is dead, just like Sadie.

"Ben tried to save her," I say again. "And then Mason went after him, too. It was self-defense." They have to understand that. I search their faces to see if they believe me.

"No one is questioning why Ben Carrera did what he did," Detective Hunt says gently. "We just need to hear—from you, while the memories are still fresh—exactly what happened. Can you do that for us?"

I nod, wiping away more tears with a tissue from the box that has materialized on the table.

"I just don't want him to get in trouble," I say, trying to collect myself. "Ben would have done anything for my sister. He'll never forgive himself that he was too late, and I just . . . Is he here now? Is someone talking to him? Is he okay?"

"Relax, Jayne. He's talking with another one of our detectives. He's okay. But we really need you to focus right now, and hopefully, you can help us make sense of what happened last night. Can you do that?"

I take a sip of the tea in front of me. It might not be good, but tea is supposed to be soothing, isn't it? Our mom, Carly, always makes me and Sadie green tea with honey and lemon when we're having a bad day. If I close my eyes, I can almost put myself back in our kitchen on a rainy afternoon, Sadie talking about the latest drama in her relationship with Ben. *It's always something with you two*—that's what Carly would say. But she just didn't understand how their relationship worked. I understood. Sadie and I are twins; I understand everything about her. Or, at least, I thought I did.

"Jayne? I said, can you do that for us?"

"Yes," I say. "Yeah. Of course. Honestly, I don't know what I can tell you, but I'll do anything I can to help. It's just . . ."

"Just what?"

I bite my lip and stare up at the low ceiling.

"Nothing will bring her back," I say finally, my attempts to compose myself falling to pieces in a spectacular fashion. "Will it? Nothing I say. Nothing I tell you. Nothing is going to bring Sadie back. And I just don't know how I'm supposed to keep going, because she's only been gone for a few hours, and I feel like one half of me has been torn away, and there's just a void. And nothing can fill it—nothing can ever fill it again because we were part of each other. I'll tell you everything I know, Detective Hunt. I swear to God, I will try to remember every single detail of every minute. But it just doesn't matter."

I look him in the eye, willing him to understand what I'm telling him.

"She's gone," I say again.

Detective Hunt is quiet for a few minutes while I pull more tissues from the box and try to take a few deep breaths. The uniformed officer places her hand on the table between us, palm up, and I put my own in it. She gives it a reassuring squeeze.

"You're right, Jayne," Detective Hunt says finally, heaving a deep sigh. "Sadie is gone. I'm not going to insult you by suggesting we can do anything to change the facts. But you're still here. And if there is anything that we can do, together, to help bring justice for your sister, then we need to try. That's all I'm asking."

He's right, of course. Sadie is gone, and I'm here. It's up to me to be her voice now. It's funny; I was always the quieter of the two of us. Now I'm the only one who can speak.

"Where do you want me to start?" I ask.

"Why don't you tell me a little bit about what happened leading up to the party last night?"

"You know, I told her not to go." Once I start talking, the words tumble out. "Maybe that's why it's just so hard to be sitting here right now. If she had listened to me, it all could have been different. If she had listened and just stayed in rather than letting Liz talk her into going—"

"When you say 'Liz,' you're referring to Elizabeth Stratton?"

"Yeah. She was a bad influence on my sister. I mean, I feel bad saying that, but she just . . . she just was. But they've been friends since we were kids, and I feel like Sadie just didn't know how to let the relationship go, you know? Sadie was too nice. Even when Liz started to spin out of control last year, Sadie was always defending her behavior. Even after what she did. I still don't know how Sadie ever forgave her."

"Forgave her for what, exactly?"

I pause for a moment. "I don't think it's relevant. And I don't want to get anyone else in trouble."

"Jayne, please. Let us decide what's relevant. If there is anything at all you have to tell us that could help, just be honest."

I bite my lip as I consider what the detective just said. Would telling them what Liz did somehow help put an end to all this? Maybe there is some kind of connection that the police would see. Something that would explain what happened to Sadie last night. Anything could be important. That's what they keep saying.

And if that's true, then I actually have a lot to say.

Starting with that time Liz slept with Ben last year.

BEN

7:18 A.M., THE MORNING AFTER THE MURDERS

"THIS IS A serious set of circumstances, Mr. Carrera."

"I didn't do anything wrong."

"We're not necessarily suggesting you did, but we're going to need a little bit more than just your word on that."

I've been sitting in this room for hours, ever since the cops showed up at Trevor's place. They know what I did. That I killed Mason. That I'm a murderer.

Jayne told them. Liz told them after she found us. After Jayne started screaming. Since they know how it happened,

I don't understand why I'm still here. I might not exactly be proud of it, but there's no taking it back.

I wonder where my dad is right now. How he reacted when he heard what happened.

"You're not being charged with a crime, Mr. Carrera," one of the detectives says. The word "yet" is implicit in the statement. "We just need to understand, for the record, what happened."

"Mason attacked her. Sadie," I say, embarrassed to hear my voice crack when I say her name. "I saw them . . . saw *him*, and I just . . . I knew I had to stop him. So I did. It's the same thing I've been saying since I got here."

There's dried blood underneath my fingernails. I wonder whose it is. I wonder if the detectives notice. There are two of them in here, plus a cop in uniform. It's weird to be treated like I might be some kind of threat. I swear to God, I'm not a threat to anybody. Or, at least, I didn't used to be. But circumstances change. Can't any of us be a threat to someone else when the circumstances change?

I ball my own hands into fists, squeezing my nails into the skin of my palms. At least now I don't have to look at the blood.

"Mr. Carrera," one of the detectives is saying—I think they told me their names, but I wasn't listening. "You did what you felt was necessary to protect Sadie Cooper. That's been made clear to us. And we understand that Mason attacked you and that you maintain your killing of him was self-defense. Can you confirm that account of events for me, please?"

"Yeah," I say, my leg bouncing impatiently, wondering what he meant by "you maintain." Do they think I'm lying? Didn't Jayne tell them what happened too?

"Yeah," I say again. "I tried to help. But Sadie didn't need me to fucking *try*." I can hear my voice getting louder, and I know I should probably be staying calm right now. Knowing that and doing that are two different things. I never understood what it meant when people said that emotions could "boil over," but goddamn do I understand it now.

"Sadie's dead. That psycho killed her, and I killed him. But I was only trying to protect her. Do you understand that? Where's Jayne? She'll tell you that's exactly what happened! She was there!"

I don't even remember standing up, but my chair clatters to the floor. The two detectives are on their feet in the same instant, and the officer by the door is on me, turning my arm behind my back and forcing me over onto the table.

"Let me go," I say through clenched teeth.

One of the detectives must have said something similar, because the officer releases me.

"We need you to remain calm, Mr. Carrera," the detective says. "We know it's been a terrible night, but you cannot have outbursts like that. Period."

The officer collects my chair, and I collapse into it. Whatever fight was still left in me after this hellish, never-ending night is gone. In place of the anger, I feel the tears finally start to fall.

"I loved her," I whisper, more to myself than to anyone in the room. "I loved her." There's a lot more I could say, but I don't.

"I know," says one of the detectives. "I'm sorry, son. With your family history, we know how difficult this must be."

Family history.

My tears stop immediately. I was wondering how long it would be before they brought that up—thought that maybe, stupidly, it wouldn't even enter into this conversation. But of course it's what they're thinking about. "Carrera" isn't exactly a common last name around here, and these guys look like they've been at the PD for decades. They were probably here when my Uncle Chris was murdered twenty years ago.

Back then the cops tried to pin it on my dad. Even all these years later, half this town still thinks Donovan Carrera is a murderer.

And now his son *is* one.

But my dad became one of the most powerful people in town. Hell, in the county, too. The cops will not be treating me the way they tried to treat him twenty years ago. He wouldn't stand for it then, and I won't stand for it now.

I wonder again where my dad is. Why he isn't busting down the door of the police station to reach his only son.

Maybe he is, at this very minute, and I just don't know about it. Hell, would they even have to tell me? I turned eighteen a month ago—me and Sadie always did something special together because our birthdays are only a week apart. I used to love being one of the oldest guys in our class. It made a big difference on the football field, honestly. But now I almost wish I was seventeen again. Then they couldn't say a word to me without Donovan Carrera looming over them. God, I wish I could get inside his mind right now. What does he think about all this? What does he think about what I did? He must know by now. Everyone must know.

"I don't see how my family history has anything to do with this," I say, willing my voice to stay calm. I already lost my shit once. I can't afford to do it twice, or even my dad's name won't keep me from being treated like a hostile suspect. "If you bring it up again, I'm going to ask for a lawyer."

My statement, and the veiled threat of getting my father further involved in this, has the right effect. I sit up a little straighter in my chair and summon my dad's swagger and certainty. My dad is a total badass. I'm sure twenty years ago, when Uncle Chris died, my dad didn't put up with any BS from these small-town, know-nothing cops.

And neither will I.

I'm Benjamin Donovan Carrera. I don't take attitude from anyone.

The detectives have been talking, and I haven't been listening.

". . . Can you do that?" one of them is asking.

"Do what?" I try to sound offended at even being forced to listen to their chatter. Their questions. That's what my dad would do.

"Tell us about what happened leading up to the moment you saw Mason attacking Sadie in the barn."

"Yeah," I say, trying to string together the events of last night in my mind. Why did I drink so much? "Yeah, I can do that. I remember everything."

"Okay," the other detective says. "Now we're getting somewhere. You have our full attention, Mr. Carrera."

"Right." I run my hands through my hair, which is a disaster. I catch something sticky between my fingers, and I wonder if it's more blood. Is it his? Or hers?

"We're waiting, Mr. Carrera."

"Right," I say again. "Let me start at the beginning."

ACT ONE

BEFORE

These violent delights have violent ends.
—William Shakespeare, *Romeo and Juliet*

"They're a rotten crowd. . . . You're
worth the whole damn bunch
put together."
—F. Scott Fitzgerald, *The Great Gatsby*

LIZ

7:28 A.M., THE MORNING AFTER THE MURDERS

"ENLIGHTEN YOU?" I repeat back to Detective Norris as I fiddle with the cap on my water bottle. "Okay, then. How far back should I go?"

The detective takes a sip of his coffee sludge. "Let's start with yesterday afternoon. How about that? Tell me everything you remember. Every little detail. *Any* detail could be of importance, so leave nothing out."

I don't need this guy mansplaining what "every detail" means. I'm not an idiot. But I can humor him, at least for now.

It's actually nice to remember Sadie. It makes me feel like she's still here and yesterday was just another normal day that didn't go so far off the rails. Like I can pretend, for just a little while, that none of this ever happened.

Of course, I'm shit at pretending.

"Lay it out for me, Patch. Sweet or sour tonight?"

Sadie Cooper appears magically beside my locker, her dark red curls dangling over me.

"Um, privacy, please?"

"Whatcha putting in your bag?"

I slide my vape deeper into my backpack, toward the bottom. "Nothing."

Sadie gives me a look that tells me she knows I'm lying and also that she isn't going to give me any more shit for it. She hates that I vape. She calls it "uncultured," although I can never quite understand how she tracks that line of thinking with the Coors Light and cheap vodka she drinks on weekends. What's that saying about the pot calling the kettle black?

"Anyway," I say, shutting my locker and slinging my bag over my shoulder. "Back to your question. I think we both know the answer to that."

She smiles. Sadie has a million-dollar smile, and she knows it.

"Trevor's?"

"Hell yeah, Trevor's. It's the first big party of the year; no way we're missing that."

Sadie nods. "Ben said Justin's definitely going to be there . . ."

At the mention of Ben's name, I feel my shoulders tense up. It's been my automatic reaction for months, and I'm not sure if it'll ever go away. God, if I'm the maid of honor at their wedding, will I be standing up there, hunched over like a troll?

Sadie doesn't notice. "Wanna come over to my place after school? We can get ready together, and you can sleep over if you want."

She says it as though it's nothing, but we both know it's become routine. I spend weekends with the Coopers more often than not, especially since my stepdad Levi started dating Melanie, a woman who somehow matches his fire-and-brimstone spiritual bullshit at a level I never imagined possible.

Needless to say, Mel (she hates that nickname, so naturally it's the only thing I ever call her) doesn't love having around the teenage problem child who, as she has actually reminded me more than once, is "still a bastard in spirit." Who the hell says that kind of thing to the family of the man they're dating? Then again, the real question is, what kind of parent lets their partner talk that way to their own kid?

Levi married my mom when she was pregnant with me, a fact that I desperately wished he hadn't shared with Melanie, even though it isn't exactly a secret. I can only imagine that her ultimate plan is to ship me off to military school (is that still a thing?), marry Levi, and pop out several of their own, fully legitimate, non-bastard children at a pace only possible with a total disregard for birth control.

At any rate, the more time Levi and Melanie spend together, the more time I spend out of the house, and the happier we all are. Probably the only thing I thank God for, much to Levi's chagrin, is bringing Sadie and the Coopers into my life. Sure, being so close with a family that isn't actually your own comes with its own complications, and, sure, those complications seem to grow the older I get, but it still beats spending time with a man who thinks I owe him eternal gratitude because he "saved" the souls of my mother and me. As far as I'm concerned, neither of us needed saving. Sometimes I still daydream about what it would have been like if it was just Mom and me. If she'd raised me all on her own, even though her getting sick would have left me an orphan at eleven years old.

"Should I take your silence as a yes?" Sadie is staring at me expectantly.

"Oh," I say. "Yeah. I mean, obviously. Where else would I be?"

Sadie nods, satisfied that all is right with the world. "Cool," she says. "I'll meet you on the steps at the usual spot."

The bell rings, and we each go off on our separate ways. I sneak a few quick drags of my vape before I step into AP US History. I've always gotten a kick out of the looks teachers have on their faces when I roll into advanced classes on the first day. They either already know about me, which means they know I'm a problem and can't believe I could actually be smart, or they don't know about me. That's almost more fun, because they assume I'm a cute little cheerleader trying her very best. The truth probably lies somewhere in the middle. Part problem, part striver. It's a gray area. But that's always where you find the truth, isn't it?

"Liz." Mr. Carson, the only teacher here who could vaguely pass for someone who cares, spreads his arms in a gesture of fake welcome. "Thank God. I wasn't sure if we'd be able to get started without you."

"Just thought I'd make an entrance," I reply with my best smile.

"Next time I expect something a bit grander. Please take your seat."

I slide into my desk in the back corner and take out a notebook. All the other kids in these classes have laptops with them, even though internet access is supposed to be locked, so all they can do is take notes. Generally, I like to tell people that my preference for notebooks and pens is just a little quirk of mine. The truth is that there is no way in hell Levi is going to buy me a laptop, and I'm too proud to check one out from the library or, worse, take the hand-me-down that Sadie offered me when her parents bought her a new rose-gold MacBook for senior year.

"I really just like to take notes by hand," I remember telling her. "Otherwise, I swear I don't remember a damn thing."

"Patch, you're seventeen, not seventy. But have it your way."

The Coopers have given me a lot, and I've always shown the appropriate level of gratitude. But there are still some shreds of my pride and dignity that I need to keep for myself. To this day, I'm not sure if Sadie believed my excuse about writing things down or if she just wanted to let me save face, but either way, I love her for it.

I really don't deserve that girl's friendship, especially not after what happened last year, but she still seems hell-bent on giving it. She's always telling me that I can't punish myself forever for what happened—that she's over it, and I should be too. But you know how it is; it's always harder to forgive yourself than it is to forgive someone you love. Maybe if you love yourself, it's a little easier. I wouldn't know.

"Right," Mr. Carson is saying, turning back to the notes he has written on the chalkboard. So help me, the man still uses a chalkboard. "Back to the delightful, horse-manure-covered world of the Gilded Age! Let's talk robber barons, shall we?"

Somehow, no matter who you talk to and no matter how many US history classes they've taken, no one ever makes it past the Gilded Age before they graduate. It's got to be promising that we're already on this part and it's just October. What even comes after the Gilded Age? I assume no teacher is equipped to talk about it, but I guess Mr. Carson feels like testing the limits of pedagogy.

"The gap between the haves and the have-nots was never so great," he's saying. "You have tenements with immigrants, living in slums, alongside the greatest businessmen of the century."

One of the guys in the class makes some trashy comment about all the sex the "greatest businessmen" must have been having based on something he read online about STDs in the 1800s, and that pretty much ends it for the class. You can dress teenage boys in blazers and ties and put them in private school, but you can't stop them from being absolute dumbasses. And in my experience, the dumbassery is only getting started. Just wait until they grow up and figure out how to really wield their power.

There are always exceptions that prove the rule, obviously. A couple decent guys. Up until the end of last school year, I would have even said that Sadie's boyfriend, Ben, was one of them. But I've never been a very good judge of character, at least when it comes to guys, so I shouldn't have been surprised that he turned out to be just as bad as the rest of them.

Too bad I can't totally forget about him. But I can pretend I have. And I can pretend everything is great between Sadie and me again. And if I keep on pretending, it has to get easier sooner or later. And that's all that really matters.

Sadie's twin, Jayne . . . She's another story. She's not over it, clearly. She's never liked me, but since everything with Ben, she hasn't even bothered to try to hide her disgust.

Or her jealousy, quite frankly. Jayne hates that I'm closer to Sadie than she is. That Sadie considers me to be her true best friend. Sure, Jayne has the necklace too, but that was a consolation prize. Half the school knows what a bitch Jayne is. She's not even popular.

Not that I'm as popular as Sadie. She's in her own stratosphere at school. People just want to be around her. I'm popular by utility. In other words, everyone knows I can get liquor into a party, and I'm pretty cute when I actually put on makeup and try, and I'm Southern. Somehow that's still a novelty around here, which seems a little bit ridiculous to me. Hell, anyone in our school could just drive a few hours and cross the border down to Kentucky and get their fill of Southern accents. But I know Alabama sounds different, and even though I could probably kick the accent at this point—in fact, I find myself dropping out of it sometimes after I've spent a week with the Coopers—I know it still does me more good than harm. And honestly, it makes me seem different. Interesting. It's the whole reason Sadie and I ended up becoming friends in the first place. For that reason alone, this 'Bama girl isn't changing a damn thing.

The rest of the day drags on, the way Fridays always do when you have something major happening over the weekend. And a party at Trevor McClain's definitely counts as something major. He probably has three or four blowouts every year. There's always one a little bit after homecoming to sort of "kick off" the year, then one over Christmas break, then spring break, and sometimes at the end of the year, although that depends on how much trouble the other parties have gotten him into so far. The police have been called to his farm more often than anywhere else in town if I had to hazard a guess, but somehow Trevor seems to find that more motivating than discouraging.

"What're they gonna do?" he says whenever someone asks him about it. "Arrest everyone in the whole damn school? Impossible. There aren't enough cops in the entire county to pull that off."

It sounds cocky, but he's not wrong. Our entire local police force might be eight or nine guys at most, and that's assuming they're all on duty.

And they're never *all on duty.*

* * *

"Miss Stratton? You were saying?"

I realize I trailed off right around the moment I said I'd agreed to go over to Sadie's after school. There's the other stuff, sure, but Detective Norris doesn't have to know everything, does he? Some of this is better left unsaid. Even I know that.

By the time the final bell rings, word of Trevor's party has reached a fever pitch. Even the little freshmen (we're supposed to call them "first years" now, which just makes me think of Harry Potter) are talking about it, not that any of them have a prayer of being invited. I find Sadie on the steps and sling my arm around her shoulder.

"You ready for this, Cooper?"

"Do you even have to ask? C'mon."

We link arms and head out to the senior lot, where her pristine white Jeep is parked next to my beat-up Honda.

"Caravan to my place?" Sadie asks.

I shake my head. "Gotta stop home and get some clothes."

"You don't have to bother stopping at Levi's. You can just borrow my stuff for the weekend."

Sadie is always doing that. Letting me borrow her clothes, her makeup, her books. Sometimes I feel like I'm borrowing her life. I know she's only trying to be nice, but every now and then, it gets to me. I just want to have my own shit, you know?

"Nah, I ordered a supercute top from Urban Outfitters that just got delivered. I want to grab that for tonight."

Sadie shrugs and starts up her car. "Suit yourself! See you later."

She gives a honk to the horde of seniors hanging around in the parking lot, and they scatter out of her way. I watch her drive off, her curly red hair blowing around like a tornado. Not a care in the world. That's my bestie.

"Are you sure about that?" Detective Norris looks up from the battered notebook he's been jotting notes in.

"Um, sure about what?"

"What you just said—that Sadie didn't have a care in the world. Are you sure?"

I shrug, annoyed at his interruption. Reliving yesterday means being able to relive time with Sadie. It's the only reason I'm indulging him right now. Of course, I just have to be careful about what I relive and what I actually *tell* him.

"I don't know," I say finally. "It's just a thing people say. Like, it was a gorgeous day yesterday, I was going to meet up at her place, we had Trevor's party that night . . . Watching her drive away, I guess it was just one of those moments when everything felt perfect, you know?"

Based on the look he gives me, I can tell that Detective Norris definitely does *not* know. This man probably hasn't had a perfect moment since he jacked off to Pamela Anderson on

Baywatch in the nineties. I bite my tongue to keep from smiling. Sadie would have loved that joke.

"I'm getting the impression you're being selective about what you're telling me," he says suddenly. "And I don't like it."

His tone has changed. For a split second, I wonder if he read my mind and knew I was laughing at him in my head.

I shrug, trying to mask my anxiety with indifference.

"I don't know what to tell you."

Of course I'm not telling him every little thing that happened. But I'm telling him all the important parts.

"You think this is a casual conversation, Miss Stratton?" Detective Norris leans forward, so close that I can smell the stale coffee on his breath. His voice is suddenly low—too low, I realize, to be picked up by whatever recording devices they have in here. And I think that's the idea.

"This feels like a conversation because I'm trying to make this as easy for you as possible," he says quietly. "I understand that your friend is dead, and you're upset. I'm trying to be sensitive with you, but that stops right now if you won't tell me what I want to know. Do you understand? This will turn from a conversation into a goddamn interrogation, and I promise you, that is not something you want to happen. I know all about you, Miss Stratton. I'm aware of your situation. And either I can make it better for you, or I can make it worse. Your choice."

There he is. I knew this guy was a complete asshole the moment I met him. I was waiting for this side to come out. Now that it has, at least I can stop trying to figure him out. I know exactly who he is, and I should have trusted my gut from the second he walked into this room.

I take a deep breath, trying to figure out how to play this. If I guess wrong, it'll be an expensive mistake.

"Okay," I say finally.

"Okay what?"

It takes me a second to realize what he wants me to say. God, grown men are pathetic.

"Okay, *sir.*"

I emphasize the word, and I can practically feel him smirking inside. If Sadie were here, she would roll her eyes so far back in her head, they would stay there forever.

Can you believe this asshole? she would say.

I seriously cannot, I would tell her.

Absently, I find myself wondering if I'm going to have conversations with her in my head for the rest of my life. Every moment we were supposed to have together, all the milestones I'm going to hit alone . . . Will I always hear her voice? And even worse, what if one day I try to hear it, and I can't?

Sadie Cooper is the kind of girl who demands to be remembered.

* * *

I'm a little later getting to Sadie's than I meant to be, but my stepdad and Mel had left me a note with a list of chores (apparently Mel is now qualified to decide what chores the nearly grown daughter of her boyfriend should be doing), and I figured loading the dishwasher and folding the laundry were not that big of a sacrifice if it meant being left alone for the remainder of the weekend.

My phone pings for what feels like the millionth time since I left school. I glance down at it just before I walk through the door of the Cooper house. It's Ben. I have him saved in my contacts under someone else, obviously. At this point, he should probably be added to my favorites, too. But that's a secret no one else needs to know. Definitely not Detective Norris.

See you at the party tonight?

I decide not to answer. "Hard to get"—isn't that what they call it? Deleting the message and tossing my phone back in my bag on silent, I step through the door.

"Oooh, okay, let's see!" Sadie screeches when I emerge into the Coopers' kitchen with the Urban Outfitters package in my hand.

We tear it open together, and she makes sounds of approval at the red crop top.

"Supercute," she says. "And I have just the necklace for that! You can layer it with your bestie necklace. We'll have to grab it before we go to Trevor's; remind me."

I make a mental note not *to remind her—anytime I borrow something from Sadie when we go out, she always ends up mentioning it to someone. Like, they'll compliment a pair of her shoes I'm borrowing or a top, and she'll make sure they know that it came from her. If I get any compliments tonight, I'd rather be able to take them for myself without feeling like I owe her one. And anyway, I have the only necklace I'll ever need. My hand goes up to the smoothed edges of my half of our little broken-heart charm.*

"Hey, girls." The sound of Jayne's voice from the foyer elicits an eye roll from Sadie.

"She must have gotten a whiff of the word 'fun' and realized she was the only one in the world who could stop it," she mutters to me. I smile, always grateful to be on the receiving end when Sadie makes jokes about her twin. It's a reminder that she and I are closer than she and Jayne will ever be.

"We're in here, J," Sadie calls back, and I slide my new shirt back into the bag. The best we can hope for is that either Jayne hasn't heard about Trevor's party or, more likely, she's heard about it and is utterly, totally uninterested.

Jayne has every reason in the world to be just as popular as Sadie. The same looks, quite literally, and the same money. She's even smarter than Sadie, a fact that they both seem to have quietly acknowledged a while ago and the only angle Sadie doesn't try to play when she's competing with Jayne.

And, damn, does Sadie compete with Jayne. It took me a couple years of friendship with her to really notice it, because it's subtle. They aren't out there betting with each other on who can run faster (which would be Sadie, anyway, considering she's up for every track-and-field scholarship imaginable) or who can get a guy to pay for their coffee first. It's the little things, like being in competition has been such a normal part of their lives for so long that it's just as natural as breathing.

If you asked Sadie about it, she'd make a joke and then tell you that even if it is a competition, she's winning. If you asked Jayne, which I sure as hell never would, she'd look you dead in the eye and say she has no idea what you're talking about. Of the two of them, she's the one I'd believe. And honestly, she's the one winning.

Because although Jayne is far from my favorite person in the world, and she's backed me into some pretty shitty corners, and there's not much I like about her, the one thing I've always admired about her is that she just does not give a damn what anyone thinks about her. Especially the kids we go to school with. And it's not even a performative thing. She just really, truly does not care.

And that's why Jayne is winning, if she's even aware the competition is happening. Because even if Sadie is dating Ben, and she's homecoming queen, and she's probably heading to Loyola on a full scholarship next year, she does all that stuff because she wants other people to think good things about her. Jayne wins by not giving a shit.

God, sometimes I envy her. Sometimes I wonder how my life would've been different if it were Jayne I'd ended up being best friends with instead of Sadie. On the one hand, maybe it would've all been exactly the same. On the other hand, maybe I wouldn't even recognize myself. Now, that's an idea I could get behind.

Jayne strolls across the hardwood foyer and into the perfect, coastal-chic-even-though-we're-in-Ohio kitchen. She's freshly showered after her horseback riding lesson, and she makes a show of dusting off the tall black boots she left by the back door and giving them a little shine.

"Good lesson?" Sadie asks.

"The best." Jayne turns and smiles, her face a mirror of her sister's, right down to the sprinkle of freckles across both their noses that would make me look like Pippi Longstocking but makes both of them look like waifish Irish supermodels. "Sundance started out a little stiff on the right side, but we worked it out. He took the course like a champion."

"Great."

"What're you up to?"

Jayne doesn't look at me when she asks. She has not acknowledged my existence since she came into the room. It used to bother me that she's so bitchy to me, but now I don't really care.

"Oh, Liz was just showing me the cute top she got from Urban. Wanna see?"

Jayne doesn't even bother trying to hide her disinterest. "No. Is Dad home yet?"

"He texted. He's running late on a meeting with Ben's dad."

"Mom is going to kill him if he's not home on time for them to leave."

It's the second weekend in October, which means Steven and

Carly Cooper are heading to Chautauqua to winterize their lake house and the boat for the season. I never thought I'd know the kind of people who "winterize" their second home, but then again, I never thought I'd meet a family like the Coopers, much less become the honorary third daughter. It's pure, convenient coincidence that their trip happens to line up with Trevor's party for the second year in a row. I wouldn't be surprised if Sadie had a private chat with Trevor to let him know which weekends were most convenient for her schedule.

It seems crazy that he'd plan an entire event around whether or not Sadie Cooper could make it, but if she would be there, so would Ben, and so would all the kids who run with them—me included. And not to pat myself on the back too much, but I've heard more than once that people are more likely to show up to a party once they know I'm going to be there. It might only be the liquor that comes with me, but, hey, I'm not above buying myself some love. I'd try it with Levi if I thought he had enough of a heart to feel anything at all.

But I'm getting tragic. Sadie is always reminding me not to do that.

"Your shit is kind of an after-school special in the making," she's always saying. "Maybe don't lay it all at once on anybody, yeah? Just kind of a slow drip of trauma. That's how you've got to roll. I've known you long enough that nothing surprises me anymore, and you know I love you no matter what, but it's just . . . it's a lot. No offense."

"None taken," I always reply. And 99 percent of the time, I mean it. But about 1 percent of the time, her holier-than-thou, Leave It

to Beaver *family-style view of things really pisses me the hell off. Before she judges my past, she really should have a goddamn conversation with her family about her own.*

"Okay, that right there."

"What?"

"Sadie's family past? What the hell are you talking about?"

I give Detective Norris what I hope is a true eat-shit smile. "I don't know, Detective. You came in here pretty damn sure that you had all the facts of this case. Which, I assume, also means you know everything there is to know about Sadie and her entire family. I can't imagine what I have to tell you that could possibly be new information."

"Cut it out, kid. Lose the attitude. This is a real investigation, and no matter how it ends, no matter if we find anything else about Sadie or Mason that would help explain what happened last night . . . it doesn't change the ending. So if you have something to say, spit it out. Otherwise, you can sit in here all on your own for who knows how long, while my colleagues and I continue the conversation with Miss Cooper and Mr. Carrera."

For a moment, my stomach drops to the floor. Then I realize that when he says "Miss Cooper," he means Jayne. Obviously.

The only Miss Cooper left.

The tears start again.

I weigh the pros and cons of telling him about Sadie's family. It matters, obviously—although, at the same time, nothing really seems to matter after what happened to Sadie. If something isn't going to bring her back, is there really any point? And what could her family drama *possibly* have to do with Mason Vreeland losing it and killing her?

"Miss Stratton." Detective Norris takes on a paternal tone at the sight of my tears. Great, my choices are to be treated like crap or treated like a small child. "Look, just tell me everything you know, okay? Leave it to us to decide what's important and what's not. Can you please do that?"

I can do that. But I'm not telling him everything. Just the parts I think he needs to know.

"It has to do with junior year spring break . . ."

SPRING BREAK

THE YEAR BEFORE

I'D GONE ON *spring break with the Coopers every year since Sadie and I started high school, and junior year was no different. It had been a particularly good year for Steven Cooper, or so he kept saying, which meant that rather than the usual Hilton Head beach house, we were heading down to Key West. Sadie and I had spent months picking out our bathing suits, and Ben was noticeably put out by the fact that even though the Coopers had made it clear that Sadie had the option of inviting him on the trip instead of me, she'd still chosen me.*

"Are you sure you want to bring me and not him?" I'd asked her.

"Of course, you know how Ben can be," she'd said, and she didn't have to say anything else.

Ben was the jealous type—he didn't trust Sadie, and it showed. She deserved better. I told her more than once that she should dump him. The funny thing is that it should have been the other way around . . . It's Sadie who shouldn't have trusted Ben.

Leading up to the break, though, things were exactly the same between them. Ben was being jealous and possessive, but he was also love-bombing the hell out of her anytime they got in a fight.

"Love-bombing?" Detective Norris interrupts me.

"Yeah," I say, trying and failing to hide my annoyance at the interruption with such a basic question. "You know, like when a person lays it on really thick to make someone feel really dependent on them. It can come across as romantic at first, but it's actually crazy manipulative."

"I know what the term means," he replies, once again looking at me in the way that I hate—like he's smarter than I am. "I was just curious about your use of it here. Do you think their relationship was emotionally abusive? That Ben was a narcissist?"

"Ben? What? No." I feel my cheeks turn red. "I mean, he could be a jealous jerk, but Sadie could be a lot too . . ."

Is this guy not as clueless and out of touch as I thought? I have to choose my next words very carefully.

"It's an expression they use all the time on a show I watch," I say finally with a little shrug. "Can I just finish my story?"

The house they rented was beyond gorgeous. It looked like something straight out of one of those real-estate reality TV shows. Even Jayne, who normally does her best to be perpetually unimpressed by everything, had her mouth hanging wide open.

"Damn, Steven," she said finally. "I gotta say, you knocked this one out of the park."

Steven was beaming.

I'd been around long enough to understand Steven Cooper's relationship with his daughters. Sadie adored him with abandon, but I could see that in his eyes, that made her love worth less than Jayne's. Steven Cooper liked things he had to work for, and I think it was probably because he'd been born the golden boy. When everyone hands you what you want on a silver platter for your entire life, it has to get to you sooner or later. I'm not saying it was healthy or whatever, but since I have my own special brand of dysfunctional family, it became a sort of game to me to figure out what was dysfunctional about the Coopers. Steven didn't—doesn't—respect people who love him too easily. I often found myself wondering how he'd ended up with Carly, who was every inch the doting wife, which I could tell was an opinion that Sadie and Jayne both shared (although probably for different reasons). Given that it was a rare point on which the three of us all agreed, we would sometimes talk about it if we were sharing a room on a trip and Jayne was in one of her particularly bitchy moods.

Carly was always a good mom, as far as I could tell, and she was a good surrogate mom to me too. But her world was so small. And she always had way more in common with Sadie than she did with Jayne. Jayne was Steven's girl. Sadie was Carly's. The two of them would spend hours planning for whatever major events were coming up at school, like making signs for Sadie's homecoming queen campaign or track meets. It was all the kind of stuff you'd want a mom to do, and sometimes I didn't know what to say when Sadie and Jayne started laying into her. They didn't know what it was like not to have a mom at all. To wish so desperately that there was someone you could bitch about. Carly was an easy target, and when I joined in, I could almost pretend that the three of us were sisters, and she was my mom too. But pretending something doesn't make it true, no matter how good you are at the game.

It was the fourth night of our trip, and I was having the time of my life. We were spending our mornings on the beach and our afternoons in town shopping, with Steven cooking up dinner every night, featuring whatever he caught on his deep-sea fishing excursion that day. I think it was swordfish that night, and it was kind of a big deal because they let all us kids have wine with dinner. Some kind of light, summery white that Carly had been gushing about. Apparently, it was a rare Italian import, as if any of us would know or care. But they had bought three bottles and decided to share with us.

I'll admit, I'm pretty bad at knowing my limits, which is one of the reasons why I quit drinking. But that night the wine just hit me like a ton of bricks. I got so drunk.

Most of the night is really fuzzy, but I do remember how much fun it was before I got wasted. How even Jayne was relaxed, probably because she was busy texting her best friend, Evan, most of the night. Carly had given up a long time ago on asking the girls to put their devices away during mealtimes. Sadie wasn't too bad about it—I was usually with her, and I think she thought Ben could just wait—but with Jayne, it was like she had to get back to Evan the second *he texted her. Any conversation with him always put her in a good mood.*

She even got up a few times to refill my glass for me in the kitchen, where the wine was left cooling in the fridge. I really hadn't meant to get so drunk. Not tipsy, cute drunk either. I'm not sure why anyone decided to keep pouring me drinks or why Steven and Carly let it go. I can't remember too much, like I said. But by the time we finished eating, I was somehow sloppy drunk, while everyone else was just pleasantly, lightly buzzed. It was Carly who not-so-gently suggested that I go upstairs to bed.

"I'm fine," I remember saying, stumbling slightly as I got up from the table.

"Clearly, you're not," Jayne said coldly, looking up from her phone with a glare that was something between embarrassment and utter disgust. I remember thinking how obnoxious it was for her to be so judgmental after she'd poured me drinks. But that was Jayne for you: judgmental.

"Mom's right, Patch," Sadie said. "Probably time to call it a night, yeah?"

"You too?" I asked, wondering why my voice sounded so loud, even to my own ears. "You're no fun!"

I knocked over my wineglass as I left the table. It was an accident, and the perfect golden tone of the wine soaked in quickly into the upholstery of my chair.

"Okay," Steven said, getting up from the table himself. "Come on, kid. Upstairs with you."

Steven was like that. Is like that. When everyone else sits around making suggestions about what to do in a situation, he's the one who stands up and does something about it. For better or worse. Before I knew it, he was next to me, offering an arm in a way that would have been gallant if I weren't a drunk sixteen-year-old and he weren't the fiftysomething father of my best friend, trying to save me from the embarrassment I inevitably seem to cause for myself everywhere I go. At least I used to be able to blame the embarrassment on alcohol. Now I have no excuse—it's just me being fucking me.

Once he helped me to the doorway of my room, Steven gave me a fatherly pat on the shoulder. "Don't be too embarrassed," he said, reading my mind. "Happens to the best of us. Get some rest."

He disappeared back to the family below while I muttered a barely coherent "Thanks."

Just my luck, Jayne happened to show up at my door about two minutes after Steven was back downstairs.

"Really, Lizzie?" she asked, leaning against the frame and shaking her head at me like I was a puppy who'd had an accident. "Your

pathetic obsession with my sister is bad enough. What, are you dragging Steven into it now too? Making him help you to bed? Do you have any shame? Is there a man alive you won't throw yourself at?"

"That's not—I didn't—" I felt my face turning bright red, and the room was already spinning. "I need to lie down," I said finally.

It wasn't even an excuse. I never even told Jayne she was wrong. Maybe she wasn't. I do have a history of throwing myself at guys. It's not something I'm proud of, but it's true.

I must have been trashed, because about two minutes after Jayne left the room, I collapsed into my bed and passed out. At the house back in Hilton Head, all us girls shared a room, but the place in Key West had four bedrooms, which meant we all got our own. I had been reveling in the privacy ever since we'd arrived. Levi isn't big on privacy, and he's gone as far as taking my door off its hinges just to make sure I'm not getting up to any "funny business" with whatever guy I'm seeing. I'm not sure if he realizes how easy it is to just go someplace else, but he seems to think that robbing me of every shred of dignity in the house is the same thing as protecting my honor, so he clearly doesn't have a very good grasp on reality.

Anyway, when I woke up again, it was maybe one or two in the morning. The whole house was quiet, with just the sound of the ocean outside. It took me a few minutes to remember what had happened earlier—how I'd embarrassed myself at dinner and Mr. Cooper had helped me upstairs to my room. How Jayne had swung by, just to make sure I knew how tragic I was, having to be helped to bed by her dad. And my less drunken self definitely clocked the innuendo in her voice and the gravity of her accusation, which was just . . . no.

For a minute, I wasn't sure what had woken me up. But then my phone pinged again, and I realized I'd forgotten to put it on silent before I'd passed out. I checked it and saw a new text from Ben. In fact, I had about six new texts from Ben.

Seriously, Stratton. What the hell is going on down there? Why aren't you answering?

I can't imagine what he thought was happening, but based on the last five texts, it seemed like Ben had decided Sadie was out at the clubs, going absolutely crazy with some oiled-up Florida boys. Part of me—a big part, actually—wanted to let him just go on believing that. But I also knew that if I let it go, Sadie was going to get a bunch of shit from him the next morning, and it would probably ruin the entire day.

All good here, dude. Chill. Your priority spot as the hottest guy in Sadie's life is safe.

I hit send, rolled over, and closed my eyes. Hopefully, that was enough to get him to leave me alone. My phone pinged again.

So you think I'm hot, huh? ;)

See, what I should have done at that point was let it go. Not even responded. But the text was just there. Open-ended. Begging for a response, like a challenge. And I could never say no to a challenge.

That's how it started. Just texting, me and Ben. I don't think he even meant anything by his response. Just him being an asshole. But

I took it, and I ran with it. Just to see if I could. Just to see if I could really be a Cooper. And so we started talking. And we kept talking. But that's all it was, all it ever would have been. I would have never taken it so far . . . until the moment I did.

But that's not what this was about. It's just important to know why I was still awake an hour later. Why I was up and decided I was thirsty.

I got out of bed, mostly just to keep myself from spiraling, and went downstairs to the kitchen to get a glass of water. In the morning I'd have to apologize to everyone for my behavior, but it wasn't like this was the first time someone had gotten a little too buzzed on a Cooper family vacation, so I wasn't stressed about it. What stressed me out more was the part when Mr. Cooper had taken me up to bed and what Jayne had said about it. Did Carly and Sadie think I was obsessed with Steven too? The whole thing made me feel so guilty. The weird part was that I probably should have felt guilty about my flirty texts with Ben, not a legitimately innocent interaction with Steven. But Jayne could do that—get a thought stuck in your head, even when you knew it had no business being there.

It was in the kitchen that I first heard the voices. They were muffled, and I realized that Steven and Carly were sitting outside on the steps of the deck that led down to the ocean. Whatever they were talking about, it was clearly intense. For a second I wondered if Steven had told her that something had happened upstairs earlier. That I had behaved inappropriately. But then I realized how stupid that was. Nothing had happened. No matter what Jayne had tried to imply to mess with my head.

My curiosity got the better of me. Since they clearly hadn't seen me and I was still drunk enough to think eavesdropping was a good idea, I decided to get closer. One of the windows facing the deck was still open a little bit, and I crouched down next to it.

"This is too much, Steven. You can't even spend one week away with your family without texting . . . sorry, what's the name of the latest sidepiece? It's so hard to keep track."

I would have laughed out loud at the idea of perfect Carly Cooper using a term like "sidepiece," but the tone of her voice let me know that obviously this wasn't a laughing matter. I'd never heard her sound so bitter.

"I told you, she's the one who texted me,*" Steven said quietly.*

"Oh, so that makes it better? Is that the rule you've come up with? It's okay if they make the first move?"

"No, no, of course not. That's not what I'm saying. And no one even made a move! You're being paranoid. She's just a girl from the office. Hell, you met her at the Christmas party last year! She was texting about a work issue. It was nothing."

I could not believe what I was hearing. Steven Cooper, cheating on his wife? Carly must have this wrong. But at the same time . . . Steven didn't sound convincing. Not even a little bit. He sounded like a defensive asshole who'd just gotten caught cheating and was trying and failing to cover it up.

"I saw the picture she sent you," Carly said.

Oh shit. This was really happening.

It was quiet for so long that I wondered if one of them had just gotten up and walked away, but I didn't want to glance out the window to check. Then, finally, Carly spoke again.

"Look, I thought we had an understanding." Her voice had changed. It sounded tired now, but resolved. I guess it sounded like the voice of a woman whose husband had nothing to say when she told him she knew the truth.

"You agreed to be discreet," she continued. "You agreed that your family would still come first. And in exchange, I agreed to look the other way. And for the record, it's pretty damn hard to look the other way when you are quite literally parading this in front of my face. When you're bringing it from the office into the house. And then we go on vacation, and you bring it from the house onto your phone for anyone *in this house to see if they happen to glance over your shoulder at the wrong minute. You cannot disrespect me and your daughters this way. I won't allow it. You do what you want on your own time, Steve. You can sleep with every pretty young woman who walks through your door, asking for an internship, who is foolish enough to believe you when you say you've—what was it you said with the last one? Oh, right, that you've 'never felt this way before.' You can have every single one of them if you want. See if I care. See if I will walk away from this marriage, because I won't. But you* will not *bring your dirty habits anywhere near this family. Do you understand me?"*

Steven sighed. Even though I couldn't make out his expression from where I was, I would bet anything that he was rolling his eyes—at least on the inside. And that he probably thought Carly was somehow the unreasonable one here.

What a bastard.

"Understood," he said finally, and Carly nodded. I watched as the shadow of her silhouette stood up, and she squared her shoulders like someone with nothing left to do but accept their reality and learn how to live within it.

"And tomorrow," she said, forcing a normal voice, "we're going to have a beach day. And it'll be a tech-free day for you, to set a good example for the girls. They're all glued to those phones. It will be good for them to see that even the great, all-powerful, all-important, ever-perfect Steven Cooper can exist without his. Are we clear?"

"We're clear."

I crept back upstairs before they came back inside, my heart breaking for Carly with every step.

LIZ

8:33 A.M., THE MORNING AFTER THE MURDERS

"SO, HOW LONG have you been carrying on with Ben Carrera?"

I'm not sure what kind of response I was expecting from Detective Norris after all that. I mean, I just gave him a gold mine of information about the Cooper family dynamic and dropped the truth bomb that Steven is apparently a chronic cheater and dirtbag of a husband, and the detective's only take-away is that I sent some flirty text messages to Ben?

"Um." I pause, unsure why I feel like the one on trial all of a sudden. "I only mentioned the texts with Ben because that's why I was awake and overheard the fight between Steven and Carly."

"Duly noted. Now, please answer my question. How long have you and Ben Carrera been getting together behind your so-called best friend's back?"

"What the hell? This isn't about that at all. I'm trying to tell you about Sadie's homelife. Isn't that something you wanted to know? There was nothing—Ben and I aren't anything. That's not the point."

"Calm down, Miss Stratton, and answer my question, or I will stop asking nicely."

It feels like I'm talking to a brick wall right now, and Detective Norris seems to have roughly the same level of emotional intelligence. Maybe less.

What happened in Key West is the real reason I started drinking more toward the end of junior year. The Coopers were the only family I ever knew who gave me even the vaguest sense of normalcy, and after what I overheard . . . it suddenly sounded like even that had been built on a lie. And if they weren't so perfect after all, then Sadie and Jayne weren't so perfect after all.

So I kept talking to Ben. Fine, I can admit that. It made me feel powerful, I guess. But then I got too drunk at this party I went to when Sadie was sick with Covid. The one where Jayne and her friend Evan showed up, and Ben and I were flirting too much, and somehow my world started spinning out of control.

That's what I would tell Detective Norris if he were someone else. An actual human being with a shred of empathy. And if I were the kind of girl who could be honest about who she really was, who could admit when she made a mistake. But he isn't, and I'm not, and so I keep the rest of it to myself.

"Ben and I were just texting," I say instead. "That's all. We might have been flirting a little bit, but so what? That's not a crime, is it?"

"Are you sure nothing else happened between you?"

"Yes."

I'm lying through my teeth.

"Interesting," Detective Norris says, scribbling something in his notebook. "And what if I told you that that isn't what we're hearing from Jayne Cooper?"

Of course Jayne told them.

"I'd say she can go to hell."

Jayne promised she would never tell. I admitted it to Sadie. Ben and I came clean, Sadie forgave us, and Jayne said that she would let it go. Not hand the fucking police a reason to dig into something that has nothing to do with any of this.

"Hey," Detective Norris says sharply. "I told you to quit it with the attitude."

"Oh, I'm sorry. I only listen to people I respect."

"You're on thin ice, kid. Enough about spring break last year. Let's get back to what happened yesterday afternoon, leading up to the party . . ."

I take a deep breath and will myself to stop feeling so defensive. This will all be over soon enough, and then I can go home. Of course, all that's waiting for me there is a stepdad who never wanted me in the first place.

Sadie and I didn't even need to ask Jayne if she was going to the party at Trevor's that night; we already knew the answer was a resounding "Hell no." It's not like Jayne never goes out, although, between her and Sadie, she's definitely the one more likely to stay in reading a book on philosophy and convincing her dad to give her a whisky to sip along with it. Jayne prefers the kind of parties you could call get-togethers. Sadie and I prefer ragers. We're in high school, for fuck's sake. If I want to sit around in dead silence and read a book written two hundred years ago, I'm sure I'll have plenty of time to do that in fifty years.

That's the kind of joke Sadie would have loved, and she would have said that we'd be reading those books together in the nursing home. The crazy old ladies always up to something.

The image is a lot less funny when I'm alone in the picture.

Jayne wanders over to the espresso machine that sits gleaming on the marble countertop and starts to make herself a coffee. Her hair is still wet, soaking through her Alo Yoga top. "So, enlighten me. What's the special occasion that merits a new top from Urban?"

"I mean, how else is she going to get Justin's attention tonight?" Sadie replies.

"Hey! I could get his attention without the top, thanks very much."

"Oh, without the top, you would be getting everyone's attention," Jayne cuts in. "Can you imagine? Just showing up at Trevor's totally naked? It's a good thing you stopped drinking, Lizzie, or that's exactly the kind of thing you might do."

I give Jayne a cold look. First of all, I hate being called Lizzie. Second of all, she never seems to miss an opportunity to reference the hot mess express I was after spring break last year. I did plenty of embarrassing shit, but while Sadie lets me forget about it, Jayne never seems to miss an opportunity to rub it in my face. And while I hate her for it, I also can't entirely blame her. She's Sadie's sister, after all. I'm sure she just feels like she's protecting her by humiliating me, somehow getting back at me because Sadie refused to punish me adequately—at least in Jayne's eyes—for what happened with Ben. Jayne has never directly mentioned it again, just like she promised, but the constant hints and jabs are almost worse.

"Anyway," Sadie says loudly. "Let's not, shall we? Jaynie, we're too busy actually enjoying our senior year to be bogged down by your bitchiness. So, let's skip the part where I ask if you're going to

Trevor's and you say no, and just get to the part where you promise you're not going to tell Mom and Dad. Cool?"

Jayne heaves a sigh. "You know going to Trevor's is asking for trouble, Dee. Seriously. If nothing else, you and Ben will end up getting some weird disease from a tick or something from screwing each other in the cornfield."

"Gross!"

"Facts. How do you think Emma Jordan ended up getting Lyme disease last year? It's not like she hikes."

Sadie laughs like Jayne just said the wittiest thing ever. "Ugh, fair enough. Look, I can promise you, no cornfield sex. Are you sure you don't want to come with us?"

I look from Sadie to Jayne. Sometimes I feel like I get whiplash trying to keep up with them. Sadie goes from being totally annoyed with her sister to being totally cool with her in two seconds. It can be exhausting.

"Are you sure you don't want to stay here and just chill out and binge some Netflix?"

"Pass," Sadie and I both say in unison, even though I'm pretty sure I wasn't even part of the invitation.

"Binge-watching is for getting through Saturday morning hangovers," Sadie says. "Friday night is for getting the hangover."

Jayne shrugs. "Suit yourself. Just promise to call me if you need a ride home, okay? Mom and Dad aren't going to be around, so it's no big deal if I have to take the car out at two a.m. or whatever."

"Oh, I'm driving us," I say. "So no worries."

Jayne gives me a look that says, despite knowing I quit drinking months ago, she does not believe a word I say.

"Yeah," she replies, arching a perfectly plucked eyebrow. She walks across the kitchen to put her empty cup in the sink. "Like I said, Dee, call me if you need a ride. Promise?"

Sadie shoots me an uncomfortable glance before nodding. "Promise."

They each hold up their pinky from across the kitchen in a long-distance pinky promise. They were always doing that, and it always irked me. This reminder that, no matter what, they were sisters. Twins. Closer than any two people on earth could ever be. And while I was Sadie's best friend, I still wasn't her twin sister. She didn't do pinky promises with me from across the room. She never would.

"And I'm serious about not telling Mom and Dad about the party," Sadie says. "You know how they were after Trevor's last party."

"In fairness, they freaked out because one of Trevor's buddies literally just left you here, passed out on the front lawn. Not a good look."

Sadie shrugs. "Hey, at least I had all my clothes on."

I know she doesn't mean it as a dig at me—a dig at what happened last year—but I still feel my cheeks start to burn.

"Oh shit." She gives me a pitying look. "Sorry, Patch. I didn't mean . . . I mean, you know what I meant."

I try to laugh it off. "Don't worry about it. And you're right. At least you did have all your clothes on."

The last time I was left passed out on someone's lawn (well, back deck, if you want to get specific), my shirt was definitely missing, and it became the biggest topic of gossip at school for the next week. To Sadie's credit, she came to my defense every single time someone called me a slut, which practically became her full-time job.

"You still haven't answered, though," Sadie says to her sister. "About keeping this between us. Deal? And I promise I'll call if I need a ride home, and I won't drink too much. Liz will keep an eye on me. She's an angel these days!"

It looks like Jayne is going through a serious internal struggle. Finally, she nods.

"Fine," she says. "I won't say a word. Just be . . . careful."

She says the last word quietly, and a look passes between her and Sadie. Jayne clearly doesn't mean "be careful" like a general warning. She's talking about something specific, and I hate that I don't know what it is. I make a mental note to ask Sadie about it later, although I'm guessing it has something to do with Ben. He can get way too rowdy when he drinks, something I'm only too aware of, and if he catches Sadie flirting with any other guys at the party—for Ben, Sadie flirting basically just means her talking to another human male—he might lose his shit. An angry Ben is not a Ben you want to see.

"Hey, girls." Carly's voice suddenly rings through the entry from the garage.

"In here, Mom!" Sadie and Jayne call out in unison. It still weirds me out that they do that sometimes.

Carly enters the kitchen, her arms laden with Whole Foods bags. From her outfit, it looks like she's coming straight from some kind of workout class, although it's impossible to keep up with which one. If there's a fitness trend, Carly is the first one to jump on the bandwagon. In the past few years alone, she's been into CrossFit, Pilates, hot yoga, barre, and now something that seems almost like a resurgence of the kind of Jazzercise aerobic videos that Sadie and I made fun of in middle school when they started popping up on YouTube.

She's borderline obsessive about "staying fit." I used to think it was just the product of boredom or a weirdly intense form of competition to keep up with the other Instagram moms. But now I wonder if she's just trying to keep Steven's eye from wandering too far off.

The thought makes me feel a little sick.

"Good class?" Sadie wisely avoids trying to guess what kind of class it was.

"The best, thanks for asking," Carly replies. "I think I burned, like, five hundred calories! Now, I've got everything you girls will need for a weekend without us. If you can turn on the oven and set a timer, you can eat like queens."

"I think we can manage," Jayne says, rolling her eyes.

Carly looks briefly hurt before turning her attention to putting the groceries away. It's not lost on me that Jayne is standing the closest to her and doesn't bother offering to help.

Ever since I started noticing the differences in Sadie's and Jayne's relationships with their parents, I became more aware of the general . . . disdain, I guess, that Jayne has for Carly. I'm not really sure why, but maybe it's natural that if you have two kids, each one will just end up being closer to one parent or the other. In my current role of unwanted stepchild, that's not something I can relate to, although I can imagine how it would be.

"Can I help with that?" I ask finally.

"Oh, sure. Thanks, honey. I'm sure you know where everything goes by now."

I help her unpack the paper bags. She's right; I do know where everything goes. Honestly, I know the Coopers' kitchen better than my own at this point, and I prefer it that way. More than once, I've wondered if I should just ask them if I can formally move in. Say a more permanent goodbye to Levi and just live in the spare bedroom here while I ride out the last year of high school. If things hadn't gotten so strange after I overheard Steven and Carly arguing during spring break last year, I probably would have asked already. But now . . . now it feels like a risk. Like if I'm around this family for too much longer, I'll end up finding out about even worse skeletons in the closet.

"Look at that. All my favorite girls in one room." Steven Cooper strolls into the kitchen and sets his bag down on the bar. "You included, of course, Liz."

Jayne shoots me a glare that could freeze ice, and I feel a little thrill.

I'm glad she's jealous.

"Y'all flatter me!" I reply, exaggerating my accent.

"You're the reason I got enough food for three instead of two, sweetie," Carly says, wrapping an arm around me. "Gotta take care of the bonus daughter!"

"Aw, thanks for thinking of me, Carly."

I sneak a look at Jayne, but she's got her phone out and is texting furiously. With Evan, no doubt.

"Okay," Steven says, clearly having grown bored of us and checking his Rolex. "We've gotta be out of here in . . . half an hour? Jesus, where did the afternoon go? I'll just run up and throw some things in an overnight bag."

"Already done." Carly smiles. "Because your loving wife knows that you can't pack worth shit."

Steven laughs. "Fair enough. That gives me time to get back to Donovan on a few things."

I watch them banter, and it seems impossible that this is the same couple who had that horrible conversation about sidepieces.

"What are you girls up to tonight?" Carly asks after Steven has left the room.

"Oh—" Sadie starts, but Jayne cuts her off.

"Just a whole lot of Netflix and pizza," she says smoothly. "Honestly, with how crazy everything has been over the past few weeks with homecoming and senior volunteer days, we're all beat."

"Yeah," Sadie agrees quickly. "Something tells me you and Dad

will be having a crazier weekend than the three of us."

"Up at Lake Chautauqua? That'll be the day."

Carly heads upstairs, and Sadie lets out a sigh of relief and gives Jayne a smile. "Thanks for that one."

"What are sisters for? I swear to God, though, you'd better not do anything too crazy tonight. I don't mind covering for you, but it's a lot easier if things stay chill at Trevor's."

I let out a short laugh.

"Something funny?" Jayne asks.

"No, it just . . . Come on, when has anything about Trevor's ever been chill?"

I realize too late that I'm playing directly into Jayne's opinion of me as a party girl, even if I haven't touched a drop of alcohol since the night we were at that other party together—the one where I made the biggest mistake I've ever made.

She levels one of her flat stares at me. God, does anyone else get creeped out by that look? It's the one and only time she looks nothing like Sadie.

"Relax," I say quickly. "Like I said, I don't drink anymore. I'll keep an eye on Sadie. We'll be home by one."

"Make it midnight. I will drag myself out of bed for you if I have to, but it's a lot easier if you get home before I turn on the security system."

Sadie rolls her eyes. "Yes, Mom."

Jayne nods, satisfied.

Sadie flashes a smile like everything is right in the world, and I am, once again, totally confused by these two. A few minutes ago, Jayne was offering to come pick us up at any hour, just to make sure we got home safely. Or at least to make sure Sadie got home safely. And now she's threatening us with a midnight curfew and turning on the alarm?

But Sadie doesn't call her out on it. She also doesn't seem to notice that Jayne has resumed openly glaring at me. Not that it isn't fun sitting in the Coopers' movie-set-level kitchen and getting judged within an inch of my life by the bitchy twin, but I suddenly find myself very ready to disappear.

"Hey," I say to Sadie. "You mentioned a necklace that would look cute with this top?"

Sadie looks at Jayne, then at me, and gets the hint.

"Yes! Oh, it'll look so good. C'mon, we'll head up to my room."

She grabs us two coconut waters from the fridge on the way upstairs, leaving Jayne alone. I glance back, wondering if Jayne is going to make a final snide remark before we disappear. But she already has her phone back out, texting away.

As soon as we get up to Sadie's room, she disappears into her closet to look for outfit options for tonight. I know the drill, so I sit on the bed and wait for her to present me with different variations to vote on. The thing is, she looks good in literally everything. She could wear a ratty old sweatshirt and still look flawless. Ultimately, we agree on a pair of baggy jeans and a tight black top. It's a party on a farm, after all, and neither of us feels like waking up tomorrow morning with legs covered in bug bites.

I hear my phone ping from my bag. I don't even need to look at it to know that it's Ben. I'll respond later, when Sadie is taking a shower or something.

Sadie emerges from the closet. "Was that my phone or yours?"

"Mine. Probably Levi calling to tell me I did something on the infinite chore list the wrong way." I roll my eyes. "So," I say, desperate to change the subject and forget about my phone, "the necklace?"

"Oh, yes! Let me grab it."

As she rummages through her jewelry drawer, Sadie knocks over her bottle of coconut water.

"Shit," she mutters. "Ugh, my mom just had new carpet put in."

I decide now is not the time to mention that this carpet looks exactly the same to me as the old stuff or the stuff before that. Carly Cooper might love to redecorate, but no one would ever accuse her of doing something "outside the box."

"It's just water," I say quickly. "It's probably fine."

"Would you mind running downstairs to grab me another one? I'll find that necklace for you."

"No problem."

I make my way down the old, curved staircase slowly and hear voices. If Steven and Carly are fighting again, I definitely do not want to walk in on it. But the voices in the kitchen sound muffled and relatively chill, so I consider the coast clear. It isn't until I'm about to open the door through the butler's pantry from the hall (seriously, who has a butler's pantry?) that I realize Jayne is talking to Steven and Carly about something. My stomach drops to the floor when I realize that the topic of discussion is Trevor McClain's party.

"I was trying to convince them to just stay home with me and chill out, but I don't think I succeeded."

"Well, they're just going to have a good time. Maybe you should go with them, Jaynie. Getting out more with the kids from school might be good for you."

"Dad, gross. No. You know why I don't hang out with those kids. They're trashy."

Well, screw you too, *I think to myself.*

"Steven, you can't honestly be suggesting that our girls go to another party at Trevor's!" Carly is pissed. "Do you remember what happened last time? This is absolutely out of the question."

I hear footsteps heading into the hall.

"Sadie!" Carly calls out.

Shit. We're busted. If I'd brought my phone downstairs with me, I could have texted Sadie to warn her, but it's sitting upstairs, utterly useless to me.

Suddenly a wave of panic washes over me that has nothing to do with the shit I know we're about to get for tonight. Because my phone is upstairs. In my bag, obviously, and there is no reason Sadie would look for it or check it or anything like that. And yet what if she did?

I don't even have Ben's number saved under his real name, but if she saw the texts, she could put it together.

I shake myself. I must be losing my mind. Sadie hasn't checked my phone once in the entirety of our friendship—why the hell would she think to look at it now? And anyway, it's locked. I told her my passcode once on vacation, but there's no way she would remember. Taking a deep breath, I push the paranoia out of my mind. This happens sometimes; I get these kinds of moments of panic. Probably the kind of thing that wouldn't happen if I wasn't keeping so many fucking secrets. But, hey, a girl's gotta look out for herself. One way or another.

What happens next plays out like a textbook after-school special. I hear Sadie coming down the stairs, and what follows is a full-on screaming match between Sadie and her parents, with Jayne interjecting now and then to add a smart-ass remark. I'm somewhat surprised that no one has asked yet where I am. It's as if, for the time being, anyway, I have ceased to exist to the Coopers. This is a family thing, and I am not part of that family. Not that I'm complaining—Levi does enough yelling and screaming at me at home, so I'm not super keen to add more of it here. But at the same time, I weirdly find myself wishing that they'd realize I wasn't there. That Steven would ask where I was, and then they'd rope me right into the yelling and whining and the punishment. The third daughter. The bonus daughter.

But every time I start to think the role I'm playing is full-time,

I get a reminder that it's really just a cameo. And who knows? Once Sadie and Jayne go off to college, if I don't end up getting into Loyola with Sadie like we're planning, I might just fade off into the sunset. Sadie will make a new best friend, and she'll realize that I was the deadweight all along. She'll meet some other girl who has a functional family, who has friends over to her own house just as often as she gets invited someplace else. Who could trade off with Sadie on spring breaks with their families so that neither of them gets too annoyed by their own parents.

And I'll be here, trapped in amber and remembering high school as the best days of my life, just like all the middle-aged guys who are so quick to buy me a warm beer or a shot at the bars outside of town.

That's what my life looks like without the Coopers. Without Sadie. It goes from a highway to a dead end, and there is nothing I wouldn't do to keep that from happening. But hell, if my meal ticket isn't the Coopers, it might just end up being the Carreras.

Honestly, it's not like I haven't thought about that. In that scenario, the one I let myself imagine, where Sadie goes off to Loyola and gets a new best friend, I sometimes also imagine her getting a new boyfriend. Leaving Ben available.

Just then the door to the butler's pantry slides open.

"Jesus!" Carly exclaims. "Liz, what are you doing in here?"

"Oh." I stumble, unsure how to explain the fact that I've just been chilling in what is essentially a closet, listening to a full-on family blowout. "Sorry. Um . . . I, uh . . . Sadie spilled her coconut water."

Luckily, no one seems particularly interested in my lame explanations. Carly drags me out of the pantry and plops me down at the breakfast bar alongside Sadie and Jayne. I know whatever is about to happen won't be pleasant, but I also feel a sense of relief flooding over me to be a part of it. The bonus daughter once again.

"Well, now that all three of you are here, I may as well repeat myself. Just in case you missed anything, Liz." Carly gives me a look that could kill a man.

"This party," she continues, "is not happening. Are we clear? All three of you are going to stay here tonight. No one is going to Trevor's, no one is talking about Trevor's, no one is acknowledging the existence of Trevor's. Do I make myself clear?"

Sadie, Jayne, and I all mumble some sort of affirmation, and Carly nods. Satisfied.

"If I find out that any of you ignored me—and I do mean any of you—there will be holy hell to pay when your father and I get home, and you can kiss your dreams of senior year goodbye, because you will be spending every spare second outside of school inside this house. No friends over, no boys over, no phones, nothing. I'll ask you one more time: Are we clear?"

We all say yes again, this time in a slightly more spirited tone. Carly can be scary as hell when she wants to be, despite the fact that she's only a few inches taller than I am. You can tell she's built from all those random workout trends she follows, and I wouldn't want to piss her off.

"Mom," Sadie says finally. "We get it, okay? Calm down. No one is going to go to Trevor's tonight. Will you please just give it a rest?"

"Don't tell your mother to calm down," Steven chimes in, breaking the relative silence he's been relegated to since he suggested that going to the party wouldn't be world-ending. I feel like him sticking up for Carly against Sadie is his way of atoning for his sins. After all, their positions are normally reversed. Normally, Carly is the one leaning into the high school fun and Steven is the one encouraging us to see beyond it. "She's right, girls. Look, we want you—all three of you—to have an amazing senior year. But this Trevor kid doesn't exactly have a reputation as a responsible, upstanding kind of guy, and I think your mother and I would both feel more comfortable knowing that you're all staying in tonight. Can you do that for us?"

Jayne nods, and Sadie and I glare at her. As if she was even planning on going in the first place. As soon as Steven and Carly leave, I have a hunch Jayne and Sadie are really going to have it out. My only regret is that I don't have popcorn on hand to enjoy the fun. I know it seems petty, but after everything Jayne put me through last year . . . let's just say I don't exactly waste any tears on that girl if she gets some of what she gives.

Satisfied that we've all been cowed into submission, Steven and Carly leave us at the kitchen bar to "think about our life choices" and go finish packing for their trip. I'm waiting for Sadie to say something, but I realize she's giving Jayne the kind of silent treatment that could freeze out an iceberg.

"Dee . . . ," Jayne tries finally.

"Not a word from you."

Sadie stands up, and I follow suit. We're halfway up the stairs back to Sadie's room when Jayne calls out to us from the landing. Well, calls out to me, really.

"You should be thanking me, Lizzie," she says in a singsong voice.

"Oh yeah?" I reply before I can stop myself. "How do you figure that?"

Jayne shrugs. "Well, you don't exactly have the best track record for making good decisions at parties, do you? It would be a shame to wreck your little sisterhood just when you've finally made up."

I feel my face burning red, and Sadie grabs my hand. Her support makes me feel even more shitty.

"C'mon," she says quietly. "We don't need to listen to her crap."

"Yeah," I reply, following Sadie the rest of the way upstairs to her room. "Yeah, you're right."

But in the back of my mind, I'm not so sure.

"Okay," Detective Norris says. "Do you need to take a break?"

Of course he interrupts me just as I'm about to get to the important part. That part about what I saw Jayne do. But then again, he barely raised an eyebrow at my telling him that Jayne ratted us out to Sadie's parents, so he probably won't even care.

And it's probably not important. I mean, how can it be? But he said every detail counts.

"Yeah, I could use a break. But you should ask Jayne what happened later that afternoon, right before the Coopers left."

"Oh yes? And what should I be asking her about, exactly?"

"You should be asking her why she took Steven Cooper's insulin medication out of his bag. You should ask her why she *wanted* her parents to come back last night. Why she was willing to do something that would force them to come back."

Detective Norris leans back in his chair slowly and smiles that Cheshire Cat smile again. Suddenly I feel like I'm shrinking. Shrinking down in my chair just like Alice when she followed the instructions on the potion that said "Drink Me." Shrinking away under his stare until I'm nothing at all.

Until I feel exactly the way he wants me to feel.

"Well, well, well," he says finally. "It looks like I was right about you. I think you do know more than you're letting on."

JAYNE

7:45 A.M., THE MORNING AFTER THE MURDERS

"SO, HOW FAR back should I start?" I ask the detective.

"Why don't you start with yesterday afternoon, and we can just see where that takes us?"

He gives me a look like I'm made of glass and could break at any moment. I'm not used to anyone looking at me like that, ever.

But nothing will ever be the same after last night.

I nod, take a deep, steadying breath, and begin talking.

* * *

I've never really been much of a joiner. It's not that I'm antisocial or anything like that. If you ask anyone, they'll tell you that I'm nice to everybody. Nice enough, at least. And I love a good party as much as the next girl, although honestly, most of what happens in our town could hardly be described as "parties." Cheap beer and bonfires aren't really my thing. They're not Sadie's thing either, really. She always had a hard time saying no to peer pressure, so she did a lot of things that I know she didn't really want to do.

"What do you say, J? Heading to Trevor's tonight?" Damian Strong has been trying to get into my pants since last year. The fact that he has now taken it upon himself as his personal mission to get me out tonight has made this day pretty close to a living hell.

"Damian, come on," I say. "It's not my scene."

"But I'm going to be there!"

"Yeah." I give him a pointed look over our physics lab table. "Like I said, not my scene."

"Okay, okay. You don't have to be a bitch about it."

"Telling you I'm not going to a party tonight doesn't make me a bitch."

"What would you say it makes you, then?"

I shrug. "I don't know, a person with taste?"

And a person who knows that if you're going to commit to something on your Friday night, it should at least involve indoor plumbing.

Mason Vreeland, sitting a few chairs over from us, lets out a laugh.

"Something funny?" Damian asks defensively.

"Just a sick burn, that's all," Mason replies, not bothering to look up from his paper.

Mason and I aren't exactly what I would call friends, but we are friendly. We're in photography club together, and although there's always been something about him that seems a little off, I've been willing to overlook it. After all, people call me a stuck-up bitch just because I'm aiming for a life beyond the borders of our little fish-bowl town. I know what it's like to be judged. The fact that Mason also happens to look like he could win a Timothée Chalamet look-alike contest also doesn't hurt. We can all pretend that looks don't matter, but the fact is that life is easier if you're attractive, even for the loner kid.

Saying no to what could graciously be called an invitation from Damian Strong does mean I have to find something else to do with my Friday night. Evan was originally supposed to come visit for the weekend, but he had to cancel at the last minute. Not that I can blame him, since he's currently on his way to Virginia horse country. Evan is one of those guys who actually does have a thousand commitments on his calendar. When he's off the map, he's off the map, but when he shows up, he is one-hundred-percent present. That's the thing about being part of the equestrian world—one of the main reasons I stuck with riding, honestly—you get to travel all over the place, and you meet the most fascinating people. Evan lives in Palm Springs, but we fly back and forth to see each other a couple times a year ever since we met at a winter break clinic down in Florida when we were freshmen. I adore Evan, because he has never once suggested that anything I want to do with my life is out of reach.

"If anyone can make it happen," he's always telling me, "it's you."

It is amazing to have a friend with that much faith in you, especially when your own family is a little more prone to dreams that exist within a ten-mile radius. I'm desperately hoping that once Sadie goes off to school at Loyola, she'll wake up to how big the world is. And realize how ridiculous it would be to come back here after finally escaping just to marry the former homecoming king and merge the family businesses.

But, hey, maybe I'm wrong. Maybe everyone around here is blissfully happy instead of living out their own versions of Desperate Housewives. *All I know for sure is that the word "desperate" is never going to be used to describe me.*

I already know I'm going to end up stuck covering for Sadie tonight. And Liz too, no doubt, although that is really starting to get old. After everything that happened at the end of last school year, I thought that Sadie might finally start to pull back from Liz. But somehow Liz weaseled her way back in. Sadie ended up forgiving her. And Ben too. I know how important it is to Sadie to be well-liked, but that was taking it all a little bit too far. It's possible to be popular and still maintain some shred of dignity. I guess Sadie didn't see it that way.

* * *

"When you say 'everything that happened at the end of last year,' what specifically are you referring to? Is this about Liz and Ben?"

Detective Adrian Hunt is clearly trying to remain sympathetic, but I can tell that he's already regretting the fact that he asked me to tell him about everything that led up to Trevor's party. Not that I blame him. I can't imagine a grown man is wildly interested in the minutiae of teenage life. But he asked, and I'm going to give him what he wants. And then some.

I knew this question was inevitable. I just can't explain everything with Sadie if the police don't also understand what happened with Liz. They need to know that they shouldn't trust her, whatever she might be telling them, and they need to know why.

"Look, I told you that they slept together at a party last year that Sadie wasn't at. But there's more to it than that. It started before that, I think. Liz came with our family on spring break last year. We went to Key West, and it was totally normal that Sadie would be allowed to invite her along. She's just kind of always been around, you know? I feel bad for her. I know it's really rough for her at home. But it's just . . . As we've gotten older, I feel like she's been a really bad influence on Sadie. My sister is—was—really worried about what people thought about her. I think Liz used that to her advantage and made Sadie think that if she didn't go to this party, or sneak into that bar, or whatever it was Liz wanted to do, then she wouldn't be cool."

"Did something happen on spring break?"

"I'm not sure. I mean, Liz got completely drunk at dinner one night. She was sneaking wine from the fridge, and it was really inappropriate. My parents had gotten this special Chenin Blanc and let us each have a tiny glass, but Liz went and refilled her glass a bunch of times during dinner and got really wasted. My dad had to help her up to bed. It was embarrassing enough just to witness it; I can't imagine actually being Liz in that situation, if she even remembers that it happened."

"Did Sadie and Liz fight about that?"

"Not that I know of," I say. "But it seemed like things shifted after that. I don't know, like my family, and maybe Sadie, started to see Liz for who she really is."

"It sounds like you aren't the biggest fan of Miss Stratton, then?"

"I don't know," I say. "I don't want her to get in trouble, but would you be the biggest fan of someone who convinced your sister to go to the party where she ended up murdered?"

Detective Hunt clears his throat and looks down at his notes. "Right," he says finally. "Right. Fair enough. So, with that in mind, why don't you just tell me whatever it is you're trying to tell me?"

I pick at the edge of my paper cup of tea. "I feel like I'm

babbling. I'm upset and scared, and, yes, I have never been a big fan of Liz's. But I don't want to cast aspersions on her. She wasn't even there when Mason . . ."

The tears start again, and I have to stop talking. I have to catch my breath.

Detective Hunt gives me an encouraging nod. "It's okay, Jayne. Don't worry about anything other than telling me the absolute truth. Can you do that for me?"

I nod.

"Okay, so the reason I brought up spring break is because I think that's when the cracks started in their friendship. Sadie and Liz's friendship, I mean. And I think it led to what eventually happened with . . . with Liz hooking up with Ben. I went to this party without Sadie toward the end of junior year. She had Covid, so she was down for the count. Parties around here aren't normally my thing, but I had a friend in town, and he was super curious to see what we do for fun around here."

"And this friend is—"

"Evan Garfield. You don't have to even bother writing his name down, honestly. He lives in Palm Springs, and he's in Middleburg, Virginia, this weekend." I already know what his next few questions will be, so I answer them. "We met on the show-jumping circuit. We've known each other for nearly four years, and he knows my family and Sadie pretty well. No, we're not dating. He's basically the brother I never had, and there has never been anything romantic between us. Unless you count a pact to get married if we're both single at forty for tax purposes. And, no, you do not need to question him."

The detective cracks a smile, and I smile back.

The last thing I need is to have my friendship with Evan ruined forever because of all this. It's horrible enough to be sitting here, going over the details of my twin sister's death with the police. The only thing that would really make it worse would be alienating my best friend and ending up with no one left to talk to. No one who understands me. With Sadie gone, Evan is my lifeline. The one who knows the real me in a way I hadn't thought was possible. And that's saying something, considering I'm a twin.

"I believe you, Jayne. We'll just look into this Evan Garfield to make sure what you're telling us matches up. I'm sure it will, and if so, then there's no need for us to question him."

I nod, feeling myself starting to choke up again. "Thanks. I just . . . Um, without Sadie . . . Evan is my rock. I really need my friend."

Detective Hunt's eyes soften. He looks like the guy in a Mafia movie who would be the one to try to do the right thing. That's the only way I can think to describe him. Unfortunately, if this really were a Mafia movie, it would also make him very unlikely to survive. I wonder what the detectives are like who are questioning Liz and Ben. Are they like Detective

Hunt? Kinder? Harsher? It's hard to imagine anyone could be more . . . courteous, I guess. And at least if I have to sit in this room and live through this nightmare, I'm going to be treated like a human being. I deserve that.

"Do you want us to call him for you?" he asks, bringing me out of the fog of my thoughts. "Mr. Garfield, that is? This certainly qualifies as a crisis, and I understand if you would feel better if you could speak with your friend."

I shake my head. "No. No, thank you. Today is Saturday. He'll be competing in the grand prix—he's been working so hard to qualify for it, and one of the other riders had to drop out for him to even have a shot. I would hate to take that away from him right now. I'll wait."

"This doesn't have to wait, Jayne. It shouldn't wait."

He's right, obviously. Dead sister trumps show-jumping competition. And yet.

"The thing is," I say, working hard to put my thoughts together, "right now, in this room, part of me can still believe it isn't real. Does that make sense? It could all just be a trick. An insane prank my sister is pulling on all of us. I know that's not true, obviously. I don't want you to think I'm delusional. But as soon as someone else knows, as soon as I have to say it out loud . . . I don't know." I look toward the ceiling, made of those kinds of big fiberglass tiles that you only ever see in schools and medical offices. I feel the tears pooling in my eyes.

"Have you ever lost someone?" I ask, still not looking away from the ceiling.

Detective Hunt seems surprised by my question, although I have to think he gets asked that a lot by people who have just had a family member killed. Then again, has anyone in this town ever actually gone through this before? I guess the last time it happened was with Ben's uncle, and we hadn't even been born yet. Who knows if Detective Hunt was here or not? Maybe this is his first murder. Double murder, to be specific, because of Mason.

"Yes," he says finally, "I have."

"Me too. It was my grandfather, so it wasn't quite a surprise. Everyone loses their grandparents, you know? And we knew that he was sick. The strange thing is, when my parents sat Sadie and me down and told us that he was gone—we were ten—I didn't cry right away. Sadie did. She sobbed and sobbed. We were still sharing a room then, and I remember staying up all night, listening to her crying. But I didn't cry at all. And I thought there must be something wrong with me, like there's only one way you're supposed to be sad. But then the next day at school, I went to tell some friend what had happened, that my grandfather was gone, and as soon as I started trying to say it, I broke down in tears. I was inconsolable. They had to send me to the guidance counselor and then call my mom to come get me early. And I suppose the reason I'm telling you all this is that calling Evan and telling him what happened will be like that. Obviously, I've already cried more than I thought anyone could, but when I actually have to tell someone who doesn't know about this . . . I just can't. Not yet."

I finally break imaginary eye contact with the ceiling and look back at Detective Hunt. The tears are now streaming down my cheeks, and I don't wipe them away. He's looking at me like he gets it.

"I know exactly what you mean," he says simply. And then he drops it. "Why don't we revisit what happened at that party between Liz and Ben in a little while, okay? Let's pivot to Mason. Is there anything you can tell me about him?"

The photography club always meets on Friday afternoons during free period. It's only open to juniors and seniors, and we all have the same study hall time, which makes it easy to meet. Plus, not that I don't adore photography, but who really wants to stay after school for a hobby? I'll take my extracurriculars in the middle of the day, thanks very much. Unless we're talking about riding, but that's in a category of its own.

I've loved photography since I was a little kid, when I became somewhat obsessed with the old Hollywood kind of still shots after my parents took us to see Gentlemen Prefer Blondes *at a classic movie night at the drive-in. That's what started it all for me.*

Marilyn Monroe, James Dean—pretty much any star who was

unbearably beautiful and died too young. It was definitely something that worried my parents when I was younger. What on earth do you do with a kid who's always watching dead stars in old movies and asking wildly uncomfortable questions about mortality? I think it was just fascinating to me. How someone could be so vibrant and alive on-screen and yet be gone for so long that they were just a distant memory. I was as obsessed with the studio shots of James Dean looking like a god as I was with the photos of his Porsche Spyder after the accident that took his life.

Like I said, Carly and Steven definitely had their hands full with me. I think they were grateful when I took up riding and started spending less time in front of the TV and more time at the barn. I was grateful too. Riding is everything to me. It forces you to be present. To exist only in the moment, nothing but you and your horse. It's curious how my interests sit at such opposite ends of the spectrum—riding is all about living in the present, and photography is all about preserving the past. What can I say? I suppose I'm a woman of contradictions.

Mason and I are side by side in the darkroom again this afternoon. I try to pretend like it doesn't bother me. The two of us being so close, with no one else around. He doesn't make any reference to his comments earlier, when Damian was giving me a hard time, just a brief "Hey, Red" when I come through the door.

"Hey," I reply, and proceed to ignore him entirely while I examine how my latest project is turning out. It was only a matter of time until my hobbies merged, and I'm incredibly proud of the black-and-

white stills I've taken of Sundance and a few of the other horses at the barn. Riding is such a simultaneously forceful and delicate sport, just like horses themselves.

I glance over at Mason, busy with his own work. I can't help but be curious. The teacher who sponsors our club is always going on about how phenomenal Mason's work is, and I honestly haven't seen that much of it. He seems like a pretty private person, and for all I know, he's taking pictures of disembodied doll heads on spikes. Okay, probably not. But I don't even know what his style is—avant-garde? Portraiture? Wildlife? He doesn't seem like the kind of guy who gets up at sunrise to capture rare birds, but like I said, Mason Vreeland is difficult to figure out.

"So," he says, surprising me by breaking the silence, "not heading to Trevor's tonight, huh?"

"I—no. Like I told Damian, it's not really my scene." I pause for a moment. "Are you going?"

"Yeah, I think so."

I wait for him to laugh and tell me he's kidding. His sense of humor is also hard to figure out. But he says nothing else.

"Oh," I say finally. "Seriously? You're going to Trevor's?"

"Yeah, why?"

"Nothing. I'm just surprised, that's all. I didn't think that kind of thing would be your scene either."

"What, the art kid can't drink shitty beer by a bonfire with all the normies?"

If it weren't so dark in here, Mason would see my face burning. I've always blushed easily, somehow even more easily than Sadie, despite the fact that we're twins.

"That's not what I meant," I reply quickly.

"Relax, Red. I know. But look, it's senior year—for both of us. This is kind of the last chance for all this stuff, you know? Before we shake the dust of this town off our feet and get the hell out for something better. The brave ones, anyway."

"The brave ones," I repeat. And for a moment, I feel a sort of kinship with Mason. Because I know that when he says "the brave ones," he's referring to himself. And to me, whether he realizes it or not.

I can never understand why so many people insist on building walls around themselves to shrink their worlds down when it takes less work to never start building those walls to begin with. Sadie is the perfect example. So much potential, and yet she's already built an entire future around Ben Carrera and the family business that looms so large over this town. She's proud of it, I know. Being a Cooper. And I guess I'm not ashamed of it necessarily, but I also don't give it much thought. I certainly don't view it as the golden ticket to a happily ever after. Just look at my parents. Sure, they play the perfect family on the outside, but when it's just the two of them, when they don't think anyone else is around, it's as if they're strangers to each other. Just two planets in orbit, passing by each other without feeling. Nothing seems worse to me, and yet I can already see my sister running down that path at full speed. How she doesn't see it is a mystery to me, but I suppose that despite everything, we're different people.

Absently, I run my thumb along one half of the broken-heart necklace that Sadie gave me for Christmas last year. It seemed a little juvenile at first to be the twins who had matching "Best Friends" necklaces. But I've always had a soft spot for kitsch, and at this point, going anywhere without wearing it feels like leaving the house naked. Sadie knows I have standards when it comes to fashion and accessories, and this necklace doesn't exactly meet them. But it's still cute, in a campy kind of way.

"What have you been working on?" I ask Mason, more to be polite than anything.

"Oh," he says. "Just some new stuff. Portraits, actually. But from unexpected angles. Like, can you know who someone is if you never even look them in the eye, if you just see some small part of them . . . ?"

His voice drifts off, and I can tell he's focusing completely on whatever he's pinning up to dry. To be honest, I'm shocked I got any kind of answer out of him at all. I take that to mean he's either too excited about what he's doing to keep it to himself, or it's such a throwaway project to him that he doesn't care who knows about it.

That's when I see it. The portrait he's hanging up on a clothespin. If you could call it a portrait—I'm not really sure. It's just a woman's collarbone, her hair brushed off to the side. It's a sort of abstract piece, with no clear focus on the person herself. I know it's a girl, because I recognize her instantly, even without seeing her face. The freckles near her neckline. The mess of curls descending past her shoulder. The half-heart necklace.

It's me.

When the hell did Mason Vreeland take that picture?

I'm so distracted by what I'm looking at that I don't realize Mason has turned his attention away from it. He's staring at me now, his eyes intense even in the half-light of the darkroom.

"I—" I'm not sure what to say, but I feel as though I should definitely say something. I'm also very aware that we're all alone down here, and even if I were to scream, it's highly unlikely anyone would hear me. And what would I say if they came running? "Help, this guy took a picture of me"? Not exactly a crime, as far as I know. But it's making me really uncomfortable.

"It's not what you think," Mason says quietly. Although I don't see how he could possibly know what I think.

"You know, I just remembered I'm supposed to meet Sadie," I say. It's a lame excuse, even to my own ears, but I have to get out of here. "I'll, um, I'll see you later."

Without another word and leaving my work half finished, I grab my bag and all but run out of the darkroom.

The basement, where the photography lab and darkroom are, has exactly zero service. When I finally escape back into the early autumn sunlight and head to my car, I see a series of missed calls and texts from Evan. For a brief moment, I wonder if he changed his mind and is calling to say he's heading here for the weekend after all.

That would definitely solve my problem of having no plans tonight. If he's around, it might even be worth going to Trevor's, just to play one of our games together. Evan and I are kind of into social engineering, just for fun—it's fascinating to see how people react to certain situations, and we'll usually make some kind of bet or another about what's going to happen. People aren't really that hard to understand if you pay attention. It's a lot like horseback riding. A little bit of pressure here, the right affirmation there, and you can predict with absolute precision what move they're going to make next.

"Hey, JJ," Evan says. He's the only one allowed to call me that. "I've been calling you!"

"I know, sorry. I was in the darkroom." I was in the darkroom with a stalker who has been taking pictures of me without my knowing it. "Please tell me you've been calling to say that you changed your mind about the grand prix this weekend and decided to come here instead?"

He laughs. "Not quite, I'm sorry to say. Just wanted to call and check in since I feel guilty that I had to cancel on you. But the invite is open if you want to come down here instead. It beats the hell out of whatever cornfield you're planning to hang out in tonight!"

"Hey! You know that's not my scene." There's probably no point in telling him that I was indeed invited to a party in a field tonight, albeit not a cornfield specifically. "There is a big party tonight, but honestly, I'd rather be anywhere but there."

"Who's going?" Evan asks.

His tone is casual, but I know what he's really asking. He's asking about Liz. He's only met her a few times—unfortunately, he's only been to visit me a handful of times—but he took an almost immediate disliking to her. He was the one who pointed out to me how obsessive she was about my sister. And he thinks she's jealous of me. I think he worries about me spending time with her.

"Eh, the usual crowd," I reply.

"Maybe you should go. You know, spend some quality time with Sadie. And keep Liz away from her."

"I literally just said that it's not my scene."

"I know, but come on, JJ. You could actually end up having some fun, even if I'm not there to judge everyone with you in the corner. At least promise you'll consider it!"

"Fine, I promise."

"Obviously, I don't believe you, but I appreciate you making the effort."

"You know me too well."

"I do. And actually, you sound a little off. Everything okay?"

I consider telling Evan about what just happened with Mason. But at the same time, it feels increasingly silly now that I'm out of the room with him. Can I even be sure, really sure, that it is a picture of me? Maybe it's a picture of Sadie instead. Although that would make even less sense. Sadie and Mason don't even know each other.

* * *

"So, just to be clear, you never confronted Mr. Vreeland about the photo?" the detective asks me.

"No." I shake my head. "I felt really uncomfortable and just got out of there as fast as I could."

"Do you think it's still at the school? We can send detectives out for it right now."

"I . . . I don't know, honestly. I left the darkroom before Mason did. For all I know, he could have taken it with him or even destroyed it after he saw the way I reacted to it. But that's why all this is my fault. If Mason mistook Sadie for me last night, I just . . ."

"You can't blame yourself for any of this, Jayne. Mason Vreeland was clearly a deeply disturbed kid. It could have been you, Sadie, anyone. There is nothing you could have done to prevent this, do you understand?"

I nod, as if I believe him. But I don't.

"Now, listen," he says, "I know this is all a lot for you, and I'm sure you're doing your best to remember everything you can about what happened yesterday. But I have a few very clear questions that I need answers to, and I want you to focus. Can you do that? We can stop talking about Mason for now. But I have some questions about Liz."

I nod again. He's talking to me like I'm someone in the middle of a mental breakdown or a kindergartner. How else do you deal with a traumatized teenager? I suppose that's what I am now, and unbidden, my mind drifts to the idea that this is exactly the kind of tragic thing a kid would put in a college essay to get ahead in one of the Ivy Leagues. Not that I'm going to an Ivy, and not that I would capitalize on a tragedy just to get an edge. That's more of a Liz Stratton move.

The more I think about Liz, the more I start to blame her. The truth is, I *want* the cops to be questioning Liz, and I want them to be tough on her. She's clever, and she's used to talking her way into and out of all kinds of trouble. I wouldn't have cared if it wasn't for the fact that Sadie was usually standing right next to her while these things were happening. God, if my sister could have just stopped putting herself in the middle of games that were way more dangerous than she'd realized. If only she'd been smarter, been more aware. If only.

"Yes," I say, squaring my shoulders and staring at the lukewarm, subpar tea still sitting on the metal table. "Ask away."

"Thank you. The sooner we get through all this, the sooner you go home. And we are going to send someone to the school now, just to see if that picture you saw Mason Vreeland with is still down in the photography lab."

I know it won't be. But if it makes Detective Hunt feel as if he's doing something that will make a difference, then who am I to say otherwise?

"First question," he says. "Is there anything you're not telling us about Liz Stratton or her relationship with Ben Carrera that we should know?"

There it is. I knew I could only talk my way around it for so long. And if I'm being honest, I want him to ask, don't I? I want him to know. I want everyone to know. The only reason I didn't shout it far and wide was because Sadie asked me not to, and even though her decision was utterly baffling to me, I respected her enough to honor that. I owe Liz no such loyalty, especially because I know it started long before Sadie thought it did.

"Last year, after spring break in Key West, I think I mentioned that things seemed really off, right? Liz was constantly partying, making the kinds of decisions that would be considered bad even by her standards. There was one night she called Sadie from Pittsburgh. Pittsburgh! How on earth did she even get there? It's two hours from here! And anyway, Sadie went to go pick her up because she was a better friend than Liz deserved. I was that hoping after that, Sadie would see it was time to distance herself from Liz. Their friendship was fine when they were in junior high, but we're heading off to college soon. It was kind of time to drop the deadweight—no offense to Liz.

"Anyway, that night I was the only one awake when they got back from Pittsburgh. Liz was still hammered, which gives you some idea of how bad she was if it was like that after a two-hour drive home. Sadie went to get the guest room ready, and I was basically tasked with keeping an eye on Liz downstairs and making sure she drank some water. She kept saying that she had something to tell me. Something about Key West and Ben? Anyway, she thrust her phone in my face and told me to just find it myself. But when I looked at it . . . Ugh, I hate even saying it out loud because it just sucked. But when I looked at her phone and tried to find whatever it was she was trying to show me, all I saw were texts between her and Ben. His name was saved as someone else's, but I could tell it was him, because the texts mentioned Sadie, using a nickname only he had for her. He called her Sunny. And it looked like they had been talking since Key West, and I mean talking a lot. And flirting. It wasn't just friendly stuff. She was always the one starting it, as far as I could tell. I wanted to ask her about it, but she was practically passing out while sitting on our kitchen barstool, and I knew I wouldn't get any kind of answer out of her that made sense. So I gave her phone back to her and just waited for Sadie to come get her and take her upstairs. She was totally blacked out. The next morning she didn't even remember getting to our house."

"Why do you think she showed you those texts?"

"I have no idea. I guess because she was so drunk? Maybe she felt guilty? I have no clue."

"Did you ever confront her about this, directly, once she had sobered up? Or did you confront Ben?"

"I went to Ben first. From what I could see, it looked like he was the reluctant one in their conversations. But also, guys think with their—" I pause for a moment, choosing my words. "They don't always think with their heads, Detective. Especially teenage guys."

Detective Hunt chuckles. "Fair enough. Go on."

"He more or less confirmed what I assumed. Liz was usually the one texting him first, and almost always when she'd been drinking. He told me that he wasn't proud of it, and it had started out harmless enough. He was just checking in on Sadie while we were on spring break. But then Liz kept talking to him, and he was worried about her—Liz kind of invokes that reaction in people, in case you all haven't figured that out yet—so they kept talking. And he let himself get caught up in it. Long story short, he told me that he would end it, and that was that. I didn't see any point in talking to Liz about it, because I figured that I could take Ben at his word. And honestly, I just wanted it to be over and done with. I knew how much it would hurt Sadie if she knew, and so I thought that if I could save her that pain by just solving it myself . . . I thought that would be better, even though I knew the truth was that she would be better off without either of them in her life. It seems so stupid and petty now. The whole time I was focusing on Liz and Ben, Mason Vreeland was obsessing over her. Biding his time. Thinking God knows what."

I want to keep talking, but my throat is closing up.

"Take a minute, Jayne," Detective Hunt says, giving me an encouraging nod. "And then I just need to know if there is anything still going on between Liz and Ben that we should know about."

Taking a final sip of the tragic green tea they set down in front of me a thousand years ago, I allow myself to go back to the night I saw something I never wanted to see: Liz hooking up with my sister's boyfriend.

"So," I begin, knowing that this is the thing Detective Hunt really wants to know, even if it does nothing to help any of us now. "One night, toward the end of school last year, Evan was in town, and we were at a party. The one I started to tell you about. Sadie couldn't make it; she was recovering from Covid. But Liz was there. She was hammered when we walked through the door, and it wasn't even that late in the night. It was clear she was going to get herself in trouble one way or another, and Evan and I tried to convince her to just leave with us. She kept saying no, and then Ben walked through the door, and she just . . . lunged at him, basically. It was clear that he was uncomfortable with it, but she made him do some shots with her, and then suddenly he wasn't so uncomfortable. I'll spare you all the details, but the relevant one you need to know is that, about an hour later, I walked into one of the bedrooms upstairs to find Liz and Ben in bed together, and they were right in the middle of it. There was no point in trying to talk to Liz in the moment. She was trashed, and I don't think Ben could've told me his own name. Anyway, I confronted Liz about it the next day and told her that if she didn't tell Sadie, I would. I told her I knew about the texting too. She accused me of snooping through her phone."

"She didn't remember showing you the texts?"

"Apparently not," I said quietly.

"And did she tell Sadie?"

"Yeah, she did. Not about the texts, though. Just about what happened at the party. Ben confessed to it too, and I thought that had to be the end of it. The end of Sadie and Liz's friendship, the end of her relationship with Ben . . . How do you forgive a guy who slept with your best friend? I mean, come on, that's almost painfully cliché. Yet somehow, I don't know, she did. She forgave both of them."

"But you never did." It isn't a question.

I shake my head and give Detective Hunt a shrug. "Come on, hasn't someone ever hurt somebody you love? Even if that person forgives them, it's so much harder to forgive them yourself. Because you saw the pain they caused. You had to clean up the mess, the aftermath. Sometimes seeing it is worse than experiencing it yourself. And when it's your own sister, your twin . . . Short answer, no. I never forgave Liz. I still haven't forgiven her, and I don't think I ever will. Sadie didn't go to school for the entire week after it all came out. And if she wasn't going, I wasn't going, so we stayed in the house." I smile in spite of myself—it's a memory brought on by terrible circumstances, but it was honestly the most fun we'd had together since middle school. "And we ate takeout and messed up my Dad's Netflix algorithm permanently by bingeing every episode of *Dawson's Creek*. It's a long series, Detective, but we just lay on the couch together, and I hugged my sister a lot, and I promised her that everything would get better. I would give anything to do that again, just one more time. But things didn't get better, did they? If only I'd known then."

"And what about Mr. Carrera?"

"I saw what happened. I don't blame him quite as much as I blame Liz. It definitely showed me what kind of guy he is, for better or worse. But Sadie loved him and wanted to make things work, so I put on my supportive sister hat and went along with it. He seemed to feel genuinely bad at least."

"What makes you say that?"

I smile, because this is a good story to tell. "He legit gave Sadie the *Say Anything* treatment. You know, that old movie with John Cusack? It's one of my dad's favorites."

"I know it."

Of course he does. Judging by his age, Detective Hunt was probably a teenager when it came out in the eighties.

"So, you know what I mean," I continue. "Ben showed up

at our house with a literal boom box playing 'In Your Eyes' by Peter Gabriel. *Say Anything* was one of Sadie's favorite movies, actually. Even though it's ancient at this point. She loved it, and Ben knew that, so he just came and stood outside and waited, playing that stupid song. After the fourth night of him doing that, even I was starting to soften up. I remember when she finally opened the door for him, and he just stood there, crying. Honestly crying, and telling her over and over again how sorry he was and what a big mistake he'd made. The two of them had big plans, you know? A big future. He loved her so much, even though he acted like an idiot. In the end, he earned Sadie's forgiveness. He earned mine, too. I'm not an ice queen, Detective. I know that people make mistakes."

"And what about Miss Stratton?"

I shrug. "I guess the reason I couldn't forgive Liz the same way was because she just seemed like someone who was saying the stuff she was supposed to say, you know?"

"I can imagine."

"Yeah." I'm quiet for a moment, not sure what else to say about it that I haven't already said or gone over myself a thousand times in my head. "Were there other questions?" I ask finally.

"Yes," Detective Hunt says, and I can tell by how furiously he's scribbling notes that the details of Liz and Ben aren't going to disappear in all this. "It sounds like you tried to talk Sadie and Liz out of going to the party last night. Can you tell me more about that? Why you didn't want them to go, and why you did end up there after all?"

"Sure. Ever just get a bad feeling in the pit of your stomach that just won't go away? Because that's the feeling I had when I got home yesterday and Sadie and Liz were talking about Trevor's. Just this immediate sense that something bad was going to happen."

"Sounds like you have a bit of a sixth sense," Detective Hunt says, the hint of a smile twitching around his downturned mouth.

He might be kidding, but I most certainly am not.

"You're not a twin, are you, Detective?"

"No."

"Well, then, it's probably not something you can understand. But twins just . . . know things. When I tell you I had a bad feeling, I mean it, and you can write that down in your notebook the same way you wrote down every other fact. I felt in my gut that something bad was going to happen to my sister. I just wish I had done more to stop her from going."

I half expect him to laugh at me. But something about the way I say it . . . the fact that I haven't had a moment without tears in my eyes since they sat me down in here three hours ago . . . something makes him listen. Or at least pretend to. Although I'm pretty good at knowing when someone is pretending. It's sort of a specialty of mine.

"I'm sorry, Jayne," he says finally. "You're right in your assumption. I don't have a twin. Or any siblings at all. I'm a card-carrying only child. So I can't know what that's like. I will make a note."

"Thank you."

"Of course. Would you like another tea?"

It's a peace offering, in its own way. I stare at the shrunken lemon slice now sitting at the bottom of my empty cup.

"Sure," I say. "Thank you."

The detective motions to the mirror on the wall of the room, and I realize it's a two-way mirror. Of course someone has been observing our conversation.

A few moments later, a uniformed officer comes in with a fresh cup of tea. She gives me an encouraging smile as she sets it down.

The wonderful thing about riding a horse is that it requires every ounce of physical and mental focus. It's the only time my mind ever quiets down, and I don't have to focus on anything except what's in front of me. I'm still basking in the peace of it when I come through the front door. The Mason situation is something that I know needs to be dealt with, but it can wait until Monday. Besides, I'm still not sure what I even mean by "dealt with." Tell the photography club sponsor? The principal? Especially if the picture is destroyed by then—something I wouldn't put past him after my reaction to it—I won't really have a leg to stand on.

But that's a Monday Jayne problem. It's only Friday afternoon.

I head straight for the shower when I get home, and when I come back downstairs, I can hear Sadie and Liz in the kitchen. Of course they're talking about Trevor's party, and I feel a knot form in my stomach. After what happened with Mason earlier, and now that I know he's probably going to be there based on what he said this afternoon . . . something about it just doesn't feel right. Not after seeing that picture.

The thing about Sadie is that she tends to overreact to things. I don't even mean in the normal teenage-girl kind of way that adults love to roll their eyes about, as though turning thirty years old suddenly erased every memory of the life experiences they'd had up until that point. I mean full-on, truly hysterical reactions. It's one of the reasons tensions are always running high between her and Ben. My mom will just shake her head and say that that's how kids are when Sadie tells us about the latest fight or disagreement, but I disagree. First of all, what sort of mother normalizes the kind of screaming, fighting, and possessive behavior that goes on between those two? It definitely makes me question how my parents' relationship started out. Second of all, I know Ben pretty well, but I know Sadie like the back of my hand. At least I thought I did. And when she blows up, she really blows up.

That's why I was so shocked when she forgave Liz and Ben for hooking up. To me it seemed like exactly the kind of thing that would be the last straw for Sadie. Your boyfriend cheating on you with your best friend? Classic high school drama, and a classic opportunity for Sadie to finally cut Ben and Liz loose in one fell swoop without owing either of them a larger explanation. Sadie cares so much about what people think, I figured it would take something massive for her to ever dream of breaking up with Ben. He's the perfect heartthrob, and the two of them are perfect together. Or, at least, it seems that way, and my sister is far more attached to how things seem than how they actually are.

But other people knew what happened between Liz and Ben. I might have been the one to walk in and see it firsthand, but it was obvious leading up to it that something was about to happen. Liz was all over him that night, and he wasn't exactly pushing her away. It wasn't the kind of thing that Sadie could just sweep under the rug (a technique she's learned to perfect from Carly) and ignore. Yet somehow, not only did her relationship with Ben emerge unscathed after his John Cusack act with the boom box, but everyone involved ended up on some kind of twisted feel-good public relations tour. Everyone was talking about how generous Sadie was, forgiving two people who hurt her so deeply, and Ben played the part of the ashamed, doting boyfriend trying to atone for his sins perfectly. Liz even took the chance to get sober. Or, at least, to tell everyone who will listen that she's sober.

Spoiler alert, she's not.

I guess I didn't realize just how much of her own integrity my sister was willing to give away to stay at the top of the social food chain. Things changed between us after that. Not in a formal kind of way—it just opened this sliver of space between us that feels as though it's gotten wider with every passing day. If we tried to fit our little broken-heart "Best Friends" necklaces together again now, it doesn't seem like they would even fit. It hurts me so deeply not to know how to cross the chasm, how to say that I almost miss the week when everything was a mess and we were just lost in a nineties teen drama on Netflix, left to our own devices.

Evan is always reminding me that you can't save people from themselves. He's not a big believer in anyone's ability to change. The way he sees it, you are who you are, and no matter how many different iterations of that you may go through in your life, the fundamentals of it will always be the same. "A leopard can't change its spots," he likes to say. "All it can do is disguise them for a while."

God, I wish he could have made it this weekend.

I've been putting on a good enough act around Liz since last year, but it's hardly a secret that I haven't forgiven her for what she did. I probably never will, although at least if it had led to my sister ditching her and dumping Ben, I could have been grateful. But I also know that Liz isn't entirely responsible for the crazy things she does. Her life is hard; she doesn't know how to manage it all. I've only met her stepdad a few times, and they were never pleasant experiences. I can't imagine what it's like actually living with the man—no wonder she wants to spend all her time here. No wonder she sometimes stares at my dad like a puppy hoping for a pat on the head. It's the only example she has of what a remotely healthy father would be like. And that's saying something, because Steven Cooper is not going to win any father-of-the-year awards. I love the man, but a paragon of paternal virtue he is not.

Liz is showing Sadie a new top she got for the party, and even I have to admit that it's adorable. Somehow, despite almost no feminine influence in her life, Liz has a pretty fantastic sense of style. It's a little too fast fashion for my taste, but she knows exactly how to dress with her petite frame to make the most of what she has. I can always tell when Sadie is borrowing something from Liz, because it's about two inches too small everywhere. Liz is barely above five feet, and Sadie and I practically tower over her at five foot nine. I'm continually shocked that Liz was able to get into the kinds of bars where she used to spend her time. Sadie and I could probably pass for twenty-one at this point, if we dressed the right way. Liz is the kind of girl who will probably look fifteen even when she's thirty-five.

"Come on," I say, sipping on the coffee I just made and giving Sadie my best please be reasonable and don't put me in a tough spot *look. "It would be so much more fun to stay in tonight, I promise. This house is one hundred percent free of any weird disease you're going to pick up in a field, and as an added benefit, you won't spend the entirety of tomorrow feeling like shit."*

Whether they decide to listen to me or not, I've had my eye on a bottle of Pinot Grigio in the wine cellar for Evan's visit that I'm happy to drink all by myself. That's the funny thing about my parents—they keep the liquor cabinet locked (ever since an unfortunate incident with Sadie and Liz two years ago), but they've never given a second thought to the wine cellar in the basement, where they have so many bottles that it's impossible for them to keep track of every single one. I should know; I've been taking them quietly for over a year, and Steven and Carly either haven't noticed or don't care. Somehow I have a feeling that my mom is the one who hasn't noticed. My dad is the one who doesn't care. He's always telling me to have more fun, and he's careful to specify that I should take that advice based on my own definition of fun, not anyone else's definition.

I ask Sadie to call me if she needs a ride home—I don't trust Liz farther than I can throw her.

"Promise," she says, and we both reach out our hands instinctively and shake our pinkies in unison from across the room. I swear, we'll be making pinky promises from afar for the rest of our lives.

It's obvious that it bothers Liz when we do this kind of thing. She prefers to believe that there wasn't really a time before her friendship with Sadie. That we all just sprang into being on the day she met us, and there was no history before. But that isn't how families work. We're all built on history, aren't we? The good stuff and the bad. But there are things between me and Sadie that no one else will ever really understand, not even our parents. We're both fond of just saying, "It's a twin thing," whenever people ask us about the particulars of the way we mirror each other. And it really is true. No matter how deep the chasm feels between us sometimes, we both know that it isn't bottomless. We both know that when we reach out our hands to each other, we'll be able to connect. The distance is only as real as we allow it to be.

I don't plan to tell my parents about Trevor's party. I mean, like I said, I have plans of my own tonight. But it kind of slips out, and I do wonder now if it's because of the bad feeling I have.

Plus, the funny thing about Carly, despite all her shortcomings, is that she has the maternal instincts of a hawk. Meaning that she could be soaring at a thousand feet, but if there is even the tiniest movement in a blade of grass from the tiniest proverbial mouse, the woman is going in for the kill.

Unfortunately, in this scenario, I am the mouse. And I don't realize it until it's way too late for me to take cover.

I thought Carly was safely upstairs packing with Steven, so I nearly jump out of my skin when she reappears in the kitchen.

"So, Netflix and pizza, huh?" she asks casually. She obviously waited until Liz and Sadie had tramped upstairs and slammed the door to Sadie's room.

If Carly Cooper is asking a question like that, it's because she already knows I'm lying. She knows things.

"Oh, um, yeah. Probably. I don't know, I think Sadie and Liz might head over to a friend's place, but I have a paper due for Mrs. Cain's class. So, definitely gonna put a dent in that and then just chill out."

It seemed like a sufficient answer. Not so vague as to arouse suspicion. But not giving anything away.

Except . . .

"And would this friend of theirs happen to be named Trevor McClain?"

I freeze, my hand halfway into the fridge to grab an apple.

"I'm not sure," I say, as casually as I can. "I thought Sadie mentioned something about them being a friend of Ben's. I don't know if he and Trevor are close."

By the time I turn around and close the fridge, I know we're all done for. Okay, more specifically, Sadie and Liz are done for—this is my one and only chance to save myself and my night.

"Okay, fine," I say. "There might be a party going on at Trevor's tonight. I'm not going, and I honestly don't know anything about it aside from the fact that one of the guys in my class asked me if I was going—"

"Oh, was it that boy, Damian?" That's Carly for you, suddenly perking up at the idea that I might have the chance to get together with someone on the same social level as Sadie's boyfriend. Which would be great if I had a brain the size of a pea and didn't doodle anything in my notebooks except my name and the last name of my current crush. I'm keeping my maiden name if I ever get married, anyway, so the point is moot.

"Um, yeah." I'm momentarily thrown off by the level of enthusiasm coming from my mother. Surely she isn't about to suggest that one of Trevor McClain's barn parties—which, by the way, led to Sadie being dropped off, passed out cold, in our yard last year for all the neighbors to see—is suddenly a good idea just because the "right" kind of boy asked me out.

You should have seen what she was like with Evan before she realized it was never going to happen with us. She practically had our entire wedding planned, and she took it as a personal offense when I clearly, loudly, repeatedly stated that there was nothing going on between us. Evan is probably my soulmate, just not in the way people normally imagine soulmates. If anything, he's more likely to try to make a move on my mom one of these days, just to see what she would do. Just to sow chaos. That's the sort of guy Evan is sometimes, and why we get along so well. Every so often, you just want to see what a person will do in an unusual situation. Frankly, that's how I view the entirety of high school. One strange, unusual, massive social experiment, and we're all just the unwitting guinea pigs. Well, this guinea pig is going to do her best to think for herself, thanks very much.

"Well," Carly is saying, "I'm impressed that Damian is so . . . persistent with you. Maybe you really should give him a chance, Jaynie. But this party is an absolute hell no from me and from your father. All I had to do was walk into Whole Foods, and I heard every mother whispering about it, so at this point, I doubt there will even be a party, or at least not one worth going to. You girls are lucky I'm not grounding you through Christmas just for thinking of going to a party like that. Don't think your father and I didn't discuss it."

When she mentions my dad for the second time, I hold back a laugh. Steven is about as clued in to what is going on in his daughters' social lives as a Labrador retriever would be on the finer points of Wagyu beef. But, sure. If it gives her more weight behind the no, then I am willing to go with it, although I don't understand how the fact that I am being the reasonable one in all this is still going to get me grounded. Shoot the messenger, much?

While I hate to admit it, I know she's right. Nothing good ever comes out of a rager at Trevor's place, and now that Sadie and Liz have been caught red-handed, I'm a little relieved that I don't have to be the one lying for them. There isn't much benefit to keeping them out of one kind of trouble just so they can get into a worse kind.

"But, Mom—" I start, more to make it seem as though I'm arguing than because I actually disagree.

"No buts, young lady. And whether you were planning on going or not, the fact that you were going to lie to our faces to cover for your sister is not okay. We raised you with more integrity than that. You and Sadie. Speaking of—"

And that's when she yells my sister's name. Our house has old, thick walls, but the voice of Carly Cooper can permeate them as if they're nothing. At the sound of her battle cry, my dad suddenly appears too. I have the feeling he was lurking just outside the kitchen until he was sure my mom was done lecturing me. Steven has never actually given me a lecture or punishment himself, although it's something he does frequently with Sadie. I like to think it's because when I get into trouble for something, it's always the kind of thing that he's secretly proud of me for doing. Sure, I bend the rules, but I do it for a good reason.

And parties like this absolutely do not qualify as a good reason.

* * *

"So, your parents confronted you—all three of you, Sadie and Liz included—about this party?" Detective Hunt asks, making a note.

"Yes. Like I said, Detective, I really didn't want to rat out my sister. My mom already knew about it, which isn't really a shock, considering how closely dialed in she is to the things that go on in Sadie's social circle. She just chose to bring it up to me because she figured that I probably wasn't going and that I would be more likely to tell the truth about it."

"Which you did."

"Which I did. And honestly, I don't know if I did the right thing or not. Because it didn't stop Sadie and Liz from going, did it? It didn't stop anything about last night from happening, and it's so hard not to imagine that if just one thing had been different . . . If I lied to my mom, or if maybe I was harder on Sadie about not going, rather than just trying to be a good sister and offering to pick her up . . . God." I feel tears start to fall again, and I realize that the tiny packet of drugstore tissues the uniformed officer gave me earlier is empty. "I guess that, as I'm telling you all this now, I'm realizing that I'm going to relive yesterday afternoon for the rest of my life. Everything that happened, I'm just going to go over it again and again and again, aren't I?"

It's a rhetorical question, but Detective Hunt answers.

"I'm sorry, kid," he says, genuine empathy in his eyes. "I wish I could tell you no, but I can't. What I can say is that it's different from person to person. How they handle it, I mean, once they've been through something like this. And I can tell you're tough and you're strong. I hope that means you'll find a way to keep on going without letting this take over your life. You deserve a brighter future than that."

"So did my sister," I whisper.

He nods. "So did she. But now it's just you left, and you have to live a life for both of you. Do you think you can do that?"

I touch the "Best Friends" necklace hanging around my neck again. I can feel the outline of the half-heart shape. I guess it's a broken heart, really, if you think about it. How do you go on when you're suddenly alone in the sky after a lifetime of mirrored starlight? When where once there were two, and now there's just one?

Taking a deep breath, I meet Detective Hunt's gaze. "I can do that," I say. My voice does not waver.

BEN

9:10 A.M., THE MORNING AFTER THE MURDERS

"DID SADIE EVER mention anything to you about Mason Vreeland?"

"How do you mean?"

"Anything that would have indicated she had any kind of relationship with him . . . Did they ever speak? Was there any reason for you to believe that he had an interest in her, or did she ever mention that they'd had any interactions that made her feel uncomfortable?"

I can feel my face burning, an annoying side effect of my

temper. Some people blush when they're embarrassed; I blush when I feel like I'm about to explode.

"Absolutely not," I say harshly. Then, making an effort to adjust my tone so I don't get smashed into a table again, I keep going. "She never said anything to me about him at all. If she had, do you think I would have let him anywhere near her? What kind of guy do you think I am?"

"We're not trying to imply that you overlooked anything, Mr. Carrera," one of the detectives says. I still don't know their names, but I can't imagine it matters. "We're just trying to figure out if Mason's attack last night was completely random or if it was somehow planned. Anything you might be able to share would be helpful. Try to think."

Try to think.

"Um." I pause, rubbing my face with my hands before I remember the blood under my fingernails. I stop immediately, folding my hands under the table.

"Okay," I say. "There is something. This might not be new to you guys—I know someone is talking to Jayne too—but I think Mason might have had a thing for Jayne. She mentioned it in passing once when I was over at the Coopers' house hanging out with Sadie. Just something about Mason always staring at her in photography club. Then, last night at the party, she said . . ."

God, what exactly was it . . . ?

"Give me a sec," I say. "Let me just—"

"Take your time, Mr. Carrera."

I nod, closing my eyes and taking a deep breath. When I was a freshman failing my way through my first football season, one of my coaches taught me this thing he called time traveling. It was a way to remember how plays went in a game, to be fully present in real time rather than focusing on the next thing you were supposed to do. That was my problem, my coach said. I was always either stuck on the play that had just happened, or I was thinking about a play coming up in the future. The key to playing a good game is to be present, and the way to do that is to freeze time. It's kind of neat, actually, once you know how to do it. You just pick out two or three details in real time and focus on those things, and then you insert those details into the play you're running. So, I would notice that there was a guy in the front row of the stands who was holding a massive Pepsi, and there was a girl wearing a hat with a fuzzy pom-pom on it, and then I would go through what my next move was in my head with those details frozen into it.

The thing about time travel is that it also commits things to your memory, and after doing it in games for so long, I've found myself doing it off the field too. For the most part, it's a useless party trick to be able to recall anything almost instantly because of the random details involved on a given night or in a certain class. But if I can dig through my beer-soaked memories of last night with enough patience, I can probably find something to tell them that could help.

"Jayne told me that yesterday afternoon she'd seen a picture Mason took in the darkroom at school. She said it was a picture of her, but she didn't know when he took it or how. Jayne and Sadie were dressed alike last night; I think Jayne might have even let Sadie borrow one of her tops. There was a second when Jayne walked through the door that even I thought she was Sadie, but I'd just seen Sadie go outside."

"What are you suggesting?"

"I'm suggesting that Sadie would have told me if there were any issues with Mason. She told me everything. But if it was actually Jayne who Mason was obsessed with or whatever, then I don't know. Maybe he got the two of them confused last night."

The detectives look at each other, and I know they're trying to figure out if this theory of mine is worth anything.

"That's something," one of them says finally. "Thank you, Mr. Carrera. That matches up with what Miss Cooper mentioned to Detective Hunt. We're going to send an officer down to the school to see if we can find the photograph. It would give us a better understanding of what was happening in Mason Vreeland's head last night."

Frankly, I don't give a shit what was happening in Mason

Vreeland's head last night. I put a pretty quick end to whatever it was, anyway.

The other detective is still talking, but I'm not listening. I make an effort to center my attention. Time travel. There is a piece of green tape on the floor near the door. I wonder why it's there. Piece of green tape, and a Sharpie smudge on the coffee cup one of the detectives is holding. Those two things should be enough to ground me here. In the moment, in the present. A present without Sadie.

"Can you repeat that?" I ask, trying to sound like the polite and respectful young man everyone expects me to be. I'm still Donovan Carrera's son, after all. Somehow, even in here, even after killing someone, I can hear my dad's voice in my head reminding me that we have a family reputation to uphold. It seems like he should be here right now, and I'm not sure if the reason I'm still alone in this room is because he isn't allowed to be in here or because he doesn't want to be in here.

It's complicated, my dad's relationship with the local PD. I don't know much about my Uncle Chris's murder, just that he was found dead by the train tracks in town. My dad was the main suspect, and it supposedly had something to do with a girl they were both dating or hooking up with or whatever.

My dad got off because there was no evidence. And anyway, what kind of guy kills his own *brother* over a girl? But half the town thinks he did it. I can't imagine what it would feel like to walk down the street knowing that most people you pass believe you killed a member of your own family.

Man, I'm glad I don't have a brother. I hate to think what I would do if I had a brother and he made a move on Sadie.

"I said, you mentioned that you and Sadie told each other everything. It sounds as though, at least by your telling, the two of you didn't have any secrets from each other."

"That's right."

"Would you care to tell us more about your relationship with Elizabeth Stratton, then?"

Shit.

I should have known. If you go slumming, sooner or later you're going to end up with a stray following you home. That's more or less how it went down with Liz, but I'm not sure how honest I can be with these two guys. They'd probably get it, but who knows how long it's been since either of them was actively pursued by a girl who genuinely wouldn't take no for an answer?

But I need to handle this. I'll tell them part of the truth. Just enough to make them understand that the thing with Liz is totally, completely unimportant.

"Look, I know it's probably been a long time since you guys were in high school, but things with Liz . . . they just sort of happened. They never meant anything, and I never intended to do anything except text with her a little bit about how Sadie was doing when they were out of town. But Liz kept trying to turn it into something more . . . If you see our text messages, you'll see that I'm telling the truth here. One night at a party last year, we just took it too far. We were both so drunk. I don't think I've ever been that drunk, to be honest. I know that's no excuse, but it's the truth. I'm a stand-up guy. I'm not going to say it was all Liz. I could have—should have—stopped her before it went down that way. But we'd both been drinking, and Liz is the kind of girl who takes what she wants, you know? That's how she ended up getting in so deep with the Coopers, getting to go on all their vacations and live the high life like she's their third daughter. I know she can put on a pretty convincing 'little girl lost' act, but she can be dangerous when she wants to be. I should know; I was on the receiving end of her manipulation. It nearly destroyed my relationship."

My eyes are burning with tears again, and I press my palms into them. *Get it together, Carrera. There is green tape on the floor. There is a Sharpie smudge on the coffee cup. You are here now. Time travel.*

"And when you came clean to Sadie about all this, what happened?"

"She forgave me. I stood outside her house with a boom box, playing this song from an old movie she loved for literally four nights in a row—"

"You mean that one with John Cusack, *Say Anything*?"

I shrug. "Sure, maybe. I don't know the name of it. But anyway, Jayne is the one who told her what happened. Jayne was there at the party that night, and I thought for sure Sadie would dump me and ditch Liz in a second, especially because Jayne hasn't always been the biggest fan of either of us."

"Why is that?"

"I can't really tell you what the deal is with Liz, although I know she's been a pretty bad influence on Sadie over the years. With me . . . I don't know. Jayne always thought Sadie could do better, I guess. And when I pulled that shit with Liz, all I did was prove Jayne right. I think it was self-sabotage in a way, because I always knew Sadie deserved someone better too. Why she decided to waste her time with me, I'll never know, but she did, and I will never stop loving her for it."

Both detectives are furiously taking notes, and I wonder how what I'm telling them is going to match up with whatever story Liz might decide to spin for her own benefit. I know my story and Jayne's will match, but Liz . . . she's a wild card.

"Anyway," I say, "that's kind of the end of the story. I messed up, Sadie forgave me, and I swear to God, I worked every day to be worthy of that forgiveness. To be worthy of a girl like that. We had big plans, you know. We were going to go to school, come back here, and merge the family businesses. Cooper-Carrera, Incorporated. Sadie was even working on some logos for us, just something to show our dads to prove that we were serious about it."

"Mr. Carrera," one of the detectives says, and I can tell by the tone of his voice that we're kicking off a new line of questioning. Great, because I definitely wanted to stay in here for even longer. I feel my leg start to bounce, and I wonder if I'm allowed to ask to use the bathroom. Just to scrub my fingernails, if nothing else. Just so I feel better. Feel clean.

"Would you describe yourself as a violent person?" he asks.

"No," I reply, without a second's hesitation.

"You're a football player, aren't you?"

"Yeah, so?"

"That can be a bit of a rough crowd sometimes, can't it?"

"Look, we mess around, and we may get into it a little bit in the locker room or whatever, but we're a football team, not a fucking fight club. And even if we were, I know the rules . . . I wouldn't talk about it."

The other detective laughs, and I smile in spite of myself. The more it can feel like we're all in this together and I'm not on the other side of an interrogation, the better. For them and for me.

"Right, of course. I'm not suggesting that. I'm just asking if your aggression on the field ever made its way over into your real life."

"If you're asking me if I ever put a hand on Sadie, the answer is hell no. We fought, sure; you can ask anyone, and they'll tell you that. But we loved each other. That was the whole reason we fought—because one of us would do something stupid, and the other one would get upset, and we would just scream it out. I'm not proud of it, but here we are. Actually, Sadie is the one who slapped me one time. She was so pissed off that I went to this long weekend thing at my buddy Andrew's house, and it was supposed to be a guys thing, but it turned out there were girls there too . . ." I'm drifting. Green tape. Sharpie smudge. "Anyway, I guess that doesn't matter now. Like I said, ask anyone and they will tell you that I might have a temper, but I'm not a violent guy. I never did more than throw a friendly punch in the locker room until last night. I didn't even know I was capable of doing what I did. It just . . . it just happened. I did what I had to do. That's the truth."

The funny thing about the truth, though, is that it tends to change depending on what the person asking you for it really wants to hear. That's why Sadie believed me when I told her that Liz and I just slept together that one time, and there was nothing more to it. She never even asked to see my text messages. She never asked for proof, because she didn't want it. And Liz went along with it for the same reason, because the truth made her look too shitty, and she knew that Sadie would prefer a clean-cut, one-night mistake. Not the conversations Liz and I were having before that night, and sure as hell not the conversations we were having after.

It didn't mean anything to me, though, and anyone who

sees the texts can see that. Can see that maybe, in some way, it wasn't enough for Liz to be a part of the Cooper family and have the benefits that Jayne and Sadie had. She needed to have *exactly* what Sadie had, whether that was an outfit or, in my case, a boyfriend. Just to prove she could.

It freaks me out when I think about it sometimes, the kinds of things Liz is capable of. She is not a girl who takes no for an answer. And I have to wonder, just a little bit, if she's got more to do with this than anyone realizes. I would never suggest that she had anything to do with it directly—I know exactly what happened, after all—but what if she found something out about Sadie and Mason and chose to simply do . . . nothing?

What's more dangerous: the person who picks up the knife or the person who stands by and watches it happen?

Without warning, the door to the interrogation room swings open with a bang. Judging by the reaction of both the detectives, they weren't expecting anyone either.

"We have a problem," the uniformed officer at the door says.

"What kind of problem?"

"A state kind of problem."

"What the hell do they want with this case? It's open-and-shut," one detective says.

"And, more importantly, it's our jurisdiction," adds the other. "Nobody even so much as crossed a county line."

"Look, it's not my job to figure out why they sent somebody out here. I'm just here because the captain wanted me to give you both fair warning. You too, kid," the cop suddenly addresses me, and I feel myself break out in a sweat.

What would a state police detective want with me? The local detectives are right; there isn't anything about this that should pique the interest of the state. It's not that I have a problem with that or anything; it's just that, here in our town, I can count on my dad's name carrying a certain amount of sway. I can count on people seeing my side of things and wanting to believe the best of me. Hell, we may even be able to keep the worst of this out of the news. I'm still a minor—can they even say my name on TV? Can they print it anywhere? I suddenly realize that my promised scholarship to Ohio State could be in serious jeopardy.

Spin it. I hear my father's voice in my head. *Whatever the story is, you spin it. You make it work. You do not fail. You are a leader.*

Okay, so what would a leader do right now? He'd keep his cool, to start.

Green tape. Sharpie smudge. We are here. I am here.

"Thank you," I say, like the cop just told me there's a fresh pot of coffee ready for me. "Is the state detective going to need to speak with me?"

"I'm gonna go out on a limb and say yes."

"Okay," I say. "It's been, uh, it's been a long night. And morning. Is there any way I can go home for a while and come back whenever he gets here?"

"You mean 'she.'"

"Oh, sorry. She."

The cop looks at the two detectives. They're clearly all trying to decide if I pose a flight risk. They're also probably trying to decide what Donovan Carrera would do to them if they held me after I asked to go. I haven't been charged with a crime, after all, have I? How long can they just keep me for questioning?

God, I really just need to wash my hands.

"We can release you into the custody of a parent or guardian," one of the detectives says finally. "I'll call your father to come down here and pick you up. You cannot go anywhere except straight home; do you understand me? And be ready to get called back in this afternoon. I thought we'd have this whole disaster wrapped up by noon, but clearly the state feels differently."

"Yes, sir," I say, feeling a wave of relief wash over me. I don't care if I can only be home for twenty minutes. I just need to be away from here. I need to take a shower, change my clothes, hug my mom. I can only imagine what's been going through her head since all this happened.

The detectives both disappear, and one of them comes

back in a few minutes later to let me know that my dad is on his way to get me.

"You can wait outside," he says. "If you don't want to sit in here anymore."

Sorry, is there a single human being who would *choose* to sit in here anymore?

"Thanks."

I wonder if Jayne and Liz are still here or if they got to go home too. I wonder if they called in anybody else. Trevor, maybe? Or Justin? I remember Liz talking to Justin a lot last night. But he was nowhere near the barn, as far as I know. He doesn't know anything.

Stepping outside feels like jumping into a cold lake. For a minute, I can't breathe. When they brought me in, it was still dark. But the sun is up now, and the air has the kind of bite to it that reminds you winter is only a few short months away. It feels good. It feels cleansing. I can separate the guy who was just in that interrogation room for four hours with the guy who's standing outside now, waiting for his dad to pick him up.

I'm not sure how long I wait on the cold, hard metal bench outside the station before my dad pulls up in the Range Rover. The first thing I notice is how slowly the car pulls up, like he has all the time in the world and is in no particular hurry, which seems weird for a guy whose kid killed someone last night. That's when I realize the answer to what I was trying to figure out earlier—whether he didn't come here because he didn't want to or because he couldn't. It was because he didn't want to. This is enough of a family scandal; the last thing he'd want to do is show his face until it's an absolutely necessity.

My phone pings three times in quick succession. They gave it back to me when I was on my way out the door, so I can only assume they have whatever they need in terms of "evidence." Not that there would be a single thing on this phone that would contradict what I told them happened last night. After all, I was telling the truth. I'd never spoken to Mason Vreeland before last night, and I can't even really call last night "speaking" to him.

I look down at my phone. Sure enough, it's her. I knew it would be, and I also know that must mean she's out of questioning. I have her number saved under another name in my phone, just to be safe. Just in case anything happened, although I couldn't have imagined that "anything" would end up being Sadie's murder. At least, I couldn't have imagined it at the start.

Were those guys total assholes to you? Because that's what just went down from where I was sitting.

One of the most important lessons my father has taught me is that, nine times out of ten, if you're polite and pleasant to someone, they will be polite and pleasant back. That's never been her strong suit—faking it like that, I mean—so it doesn't surprise me that her experience with the detectives was a little different from mine.

They were ok. Out now, my dad just pulled up. We'll talk soon.

Glancing up, I wonder what's taking him so long to get out of the car, or at the very least open the window and wave me over if he doesn't want his face to be seen. But that's the moment I realize something. It isn't my dad's Range Rover. It belongs to someone else entirely. And that someone is getting out now, cigarette in her mouth and a cup of coffee in her hand. She looks better than just about every woman her age in this town, and I'd guess she's about forty-five or so. That's how I know she must not be from around here. I watch as she tosses the cigarette on the ground by the car and stomps it out impatiently.

I've always had a thing for older women. When they're hot, I mean.

Instinctively, I smooth my wrinkled shirt and try to adjust the way I'm sitting on the bench outside. Trying to look like . . . like what? Like I didn't just get out of four hours of questioning for killing the guy who killed my girlfriend? Trying to look like the kind of stand-up guy who a woman like that could ask for directions or lean on in case she's here to handle some difficult business?

Smooth, Carrera. Very smooth.

When she gets to the doors of the police station, she pauses for a moment. I can tell that she's giving it some thought, "it" being whatever it is she has to do once she goes in there. She has light brown hair and an outfit that makes it look like she's showing up for a business meeting in Washington, DC, not a small town in Ohio. Maybe she's in from out of town to identify a body or report some kind of crime across state lines. Vaguely, I hope to God she isn't a member of the Vreeland family. That's not a level of awkward I can handle right now.

Given that there's still no sign of my dad in our Range Rover, I bite. I can't just leave her standing here, dithering about whether or not she should go inside.

"Um, excuse me, ma'am," I say, standing up. She looks surprised, as if she hadn't even noticed I was sitting there. "Can I help you? Do you need somebody to come in there with you?"

She sizes me up, and a look of recognition seems to flash over her face, but it's gone in an instant.

"Actually," she says, "yes. I would appreciate that."

"Of course," I reply, giving her the kindest smile I can muster. I hold open the door and follow behind her as she walks inside. I figure I can at least wait until the officer at the reception desk directs her to the place she's looking for, then go back outside and call my dad to ask him if he's even going to bother showing up at all or if I should walk home.

To my surprise, the cop at the desk seems to recognize her.

"Well, well, well," he says, standing up and shaking her

hand through the slot in the bulletproof protective glass. "Never thought I'd see you around these parts again."

"You know how it goes. When duty calls . . ."

"Oh, I know how it is." His voice is dripping with sarcasm.

The woman shrugs it off. "Listen, I'm here on official business, which you probably already know. Can you get me a room, please?"

"Of course. Terrible what happened with those kids."

She nods. "Terrible."

Then, turning toward me and tilting her perfect face up as though she's just recalled I'm standing there, she gives me a smile. "Terrible," she says again. "Isn't it, Mr. Carrera?"

Fuck.

"I, um, I'm not—" I feel like I've been caught with my dick in my hand.

"That's what I thought," she says, extending a hand. "Detective Sloane Budd, state police. Nice to meet you, Ben."

At a loss as to what else to do, I shake the hand she offers.

"I know you were on your way out the door," she says casually, putting a surprisingly strong hand on my shoulder, "but I'm afraid I have a few more questions for you."

"Oh," I say, conscious that I'm already being led back toward the interrogation room I just escaped ten minutes ago. "I already told the guys in there everything I know."

"I'm sure you did," Detective Budd replies, giving me a

friendly smile. "But I'm not with the local police, and frankly, I don't give a damn what you told them. I'm here now, and that means you will be explaining yourself to me. Are we clear?"

"Yes, ma'am."

It's clear that Sloane Budd means business. It's also clear that if I can't talk my way around this woman, I am absolutely, completely fucked.

Because she wants the truth, and she's not going to get it from me.

At that moment, my phone pings again.

"Oh," she says. "Phone back and everything, huh? They must have really rolled out the red carpet for you."

A uniformed officer unlocks the door of the interrogation room for us, and she guides me inside.

"I'll just go ahead and take that," she says, holding out her hand.

"Can I see some identification or something?" I ask, finally finding some balls. "Before I hand it over. I know who you said you are, but I haven't seen any proof."

"Oh, of course," she replies. "Where are my manners?"

She takes out her badge and flashes it in front of my face. "There. Happy?"

"Happy" isn't exactly how I would describe my current feeling. But if she's trying to scare the shit out of me, it might be working.

Because talking my way out of questions from our local PD is one thing. But I can already tell that talking my way out of questions from this bitch is going to be a different game entirely.

It's the kind of game my father might be up for, but the whole problem is that I'm still not Donovan Carrera.

LIZ

10:15 A.M., THE MORNING AFTER THE MURDERS

I'M NOT SURE what I'm expecting when the door to the interrogation room opens again. (Is it an interrogation room? That's sure what it feels like, although I'm sure the cops have some kind of polite name for it now.) Detective Norris walked out the door about ten minutes ago, after the woman in uniform who brought me a water came in and whispered something in his ear. Whatever it was, it pissed him off so much that he knocked his own chair over when he stood up.

He left about two minutes later, and I can't say I miss the

guy. He really thought he had me figured out, and I fucking hate being treated like that. Like some kind of stereotype. I can see it all through his eyes, obviously. I'm not an idiot, and I know the fact that Ben and I have been texting on and off for nearly six months makes me look really bad. Thirsty, even. But it's so much more complicated than that, and he hasn't even given me a chance to explain myself. I feel like I'm already on trial, and I don't even know what the charge is yet.

Don't you? I hear the voice in the back of my mind, but I shut it down. Now is not the time.

Because the door is opening again, and in walks someone who is definitively *not* Detective Norris. Or anybody I've seen around the station at all. She looks like an extra on one of those TV shows about billionaire businesspeople, and I have no idea what she's doing here.

"Elizabeth Stratton?" she asks, taking a seat and sliding over a McDonald's bag. It smells so good, I think I might throw up.

"Um—"

"It's not a trick question. You get the Egg McMuffin either way."

Tentatively, I open the bag and look inside.

"Is there a hash brown in here too?"

"Yup."

I look from the bag to the large dark eyes of the woman sitting across from me. I still don't know who she is, and I have no reason to trust her any more than I trust Detective Norris, except for the fact that she doesn't creep me the hell out. And she brought me food. And like it or not, I'm starving. It's increasingly clear that I'm not getting out of here anytime soon—especially if they just brought in someone new to take over the questioning—so eating a little something can't hurt.

"You sure I can just . . . have this?" I ask.

"Yes. I'm sure. And I'm Detective Budd, by the way. Sloane Budd. I'm here on special interest from the state."

"Shit."

"Yeah, something like that. Listen, I know it's already been a long morning for you, and I also know that you're not of much use to me unless you've been fed and watered. Hence the peace offering, if you want to call it that. I just want to shoot straight with you from the start. And my hope is that, once you've had some breakfast, you and I can have a conversation a bit more productive than the one you were having with Detective Norris. So, what do you say? Do we have a deal?"

"I don't know if there's much else I can tell you about what happened that I didn't already tell the other guy."

"That's fine. I'm not going to be asking you the same kinds of questions."

I should definitely care about what this woman is saying. She's in from the state, although I can't imagine why, and if she's taking over, then clearly something has gone wrong. More wrong than it already has, anyway. But if I'm being honest, I'm too tired and hungry to care right now. She's right; I'm not much good to anyone if I can barely see straight. Not that food is going to solve that. After last night, I honestly don't know how I'll ever see straight again.

"Stop looking at the bag like I poisoned it," Detective Budd says. "Either eat it or don't, but you should know that me bringing you food doesn't mean that I'm predisposed to further favors."

"Yes, ma'am," I reply, and even I'm surprised at the lack of irony in my voice. Whoever this woman is, I respect her a hell of a lot more than the assholes in the local PD.

So, screw it, I'm eating the McMuffin. And the hash brown. And I'm even going to drink the shitty coffee that comes along with it. (*Sellout*, I can hear Sadie saying, giving me crap for slumming it on the coffee front when I'm such a pretentious barista now.)

It takes me all of about two minutes to inhale the entire contents of the bag. I honestly didn't realize how hungry I was or that I could even manage to eat again after last night. I wonder if that's how it's going to be—having no idea how I'm going to do the basic shit in my daily life without Sadie and then just . . . doing it. Barely thinking about it.

A wave of guilt washes over me. Good. I shouldn't be

doing anything without feeling guilty. I shouldn't be *breathing* without feeling guilty.

"Okay," Detective Budd says, giving me the dignity of swallowing my last bite and washing it down with a sip of scalding coffee. "So. Food for the truth. Now that you've had the food, why don't you start telling the truth?"

"I've already told Detective Norris everything he wanted to know."

"Yeah . . . Funny thing about him, he wanted to know all the wrong things."

"How do you know?"

"I read his notes. You're pretty damn feisty, by the way. I respect that. No one here has given you a reason to trust them, and you're just acting accordingly."

"So, what about you?"

"What about me?"

"Are you suggesting that I should be trusting you instead of the local guys?"

"This is a murder investigation, Miss Stratton. To be frank, you shouldn't be trusting anyone. I certainly don't, and that includes you. So, you make up your own mind about whether or not you're going to trust me. If it helps, I read your file, and it sounds like the two of us have something in common when it comes to our childhoods. My family dynamic wasn't exactly a shining paragon of domestic bliss. You make of that what you will, but what I can promise you is that I'm here to listen to you. What happens after that depends a lot on what you have to say."

I nod. That makes sense. And even if mentioning her own shitty childhood is just a tactic, at least it's a tactic I can appreciate. Girls like that—like me, like this detective, if she's telling the truth—know how to do what it takes to get by. That's not something most people can understand if they haven't been through it themselves.

So maybe Detective Budd will really listen. Maybe I can tell her everything.

Or almost everything.

ACT TWO

THE NIGHT OF THE PARTY

Dreamers often lie.

—William Shakespeare, *Romeo and Juliet*

I like large parties. They're so intimate.
At small parties there isn't any privacy.

—F. Scott Fitzgerald, *The Great Gatsby*

LIZ

"WHAT THE HELL, *Jayne?"*

Normally, I try not to be actively bitchy toward Sadie's sister in front of her. I know she doesn't like the fact that Jayne and I don't get along, and more often than not, she probably just feels like she's stuck in the middle. But I can't help it; I'm pissed.

"It was an accident, okay? And besides, Carly pretty much already knew Trevor was having a party."

"I don't buy it. You just didn't want us to go out tonight, so you waited until we weren't around and just conveniently let it slip."

Jayne rolls her eyes. "Believe it or not, Lizzie, I don't really care what you do. I was looking forward to having the house to myself."

Sadie gives her a look. I know that look. She's not buying it.

"Did you invite someone over or something? Is it that college guy you've been texting?"

"He's been texting me," Jayne replies. "He's hot, but beyond that he's a bore."

It doesn't escape my attention that Jayne didn't actually answer Sadie's question.

"Wait, since when?" Sadie demands. "I thought you were kind of into him?"

I start to tune them out. I don't care who Jayne may or may not be texting; what I really care about is that our Friday-night plans just got completely destroyed, and it's all because Jayne picked this particular afternoon to be a snitch. Honestly, I'm not sure if this college guy is even real. Jayne makes shit up all the time, if you ask me. But of course Sadie is all in and seems to have already forgotten she was mad at Jayne.

"Listen," Jayne says, leaning forward on the kitchen counter. Sadie and I lean in too.

"I feel really bad about this. Carly and Steven are going to be out of here as soon as they finish getting their stuff together. They trust me—no offense, Dee." Sadie shrugs. I know she doesn't mind. Jayne has always been the more responsible of the two of them. The one more likely to be left in charge. She is, after all, the

"older" sister. Even if the difference is only three minutes.

"Anyway," Jayne continues, "I'll cover for you guys tonight. If you want to go. I still think it's a bad idea, but I was kind of hoping you'd reach that conclusion on your own."

God, she sounds so much like a parent sometimes.

"So, before you go, we'll just take some photos of us chilling out with a pizza or whatever, and then you can go, and we can send those to Mom and Dad if they text to check up on us. Cool?"

Sadie looks ready to agree on the spot, but I don't trust Jayne. She must have an angle.

"Why are you doing this?" I ask, not bothering to hide the suspicion from my voice.

"Because it's senior year, and I know you guys probably don't have that much time left together before you go your separate ways for school. And like I said, I made my own plans tonight, and they really don't include the two of you also being home . . ."

The dig isn't lost on me—what Jayne said about me and Sadie not having much time left together before going our "separate ways." She knows I'm applying to Loyola too. She just doesn't think I'm going to get in.

"Come on, Liz," Sadie says. "Just take the win. Let's go out tonight and have fun. Jaynie can stay here and have her own kind of fun." Sadie gives her sister a wink. "I mean, what are we going to do? Stay home based on the principle of the thing?"

She's right, of course.

"Okay, okay," I say. "Besides, my new top is too cute not to be seen."

"That's my Patch!" Sadie says, throwing an arm around me.

"You seem to deeply distrust Jayne Cooper."

Detective Budd has been listening intently. It's a nice change, actually, to feel like an adult is listening to me.

"I mean, yeah. Didn't that Norris guy tell you what I told him?"

"About Jayne going through Steven Cooper's things?"

"Yeah. I'm telling you, she took his medication out of his bag."

"And why would she do that? You just said that she had her own plans last night. Sounds like some guy was coming over. Surely she wouldn't want her parents walking back in on that?"

"I don't know why she did it. I'm just telling you, that's what I saw."

"Okay." Detective Budd makes a note. "I understand that's what you believe you saw. I promise you I will ask Jayne about it."

"You're talking to her too?" I ask, wishing my voice didn't sound so nervous.

"Yes. I'm speaking to you, Jayne Cooper, and Ben Carrera. I asked for full access to this case, Miss Stratton. That's how you make sure nothing gets lost in the shuffle."

Lost in the shuffle . . . That statement should make me feel better, but somehow it only makes me feel worse.

"I'd like to switch gears for a moment, if we could," she continues.

"Um, okay."

"Can you tell me a little bit about how you met Sadie? The two of you clearly had an incredibly strong bond. I understand you've been friends for a long time, and I'd like to hear more about that."

"What does that have to do with what happened?"

"I just want to get to know you better, Miss Stratton. And I need to get to know Sadie better too. She may be gone now, but she still has a lot to say. The best way I can figure out what that might be is by talking to the people who knew her best. You're one of them."

Well, she's right about that. I probably know—knew—Sadie better than anyone. Even Jayne, even Ben. Definitely her own parents. And it feels nice to be asked a question that doesn't make me feel like I'm being pushed into a corner.

"Okay," I say. "Yeah. The first thing you need to know, which I guess you probably already know by now, is that my stepdad Levi and I moved here when I was twelve. That's a really shitty age to move, and I had a hard time my first few weeks at school here. Everyone was making fun of my accent, and I didn't have the right clothes or know the right slang or whatever. It was tough. Anyway, I noticed that there was this one girl in my social studies class who was always staring at me.

Not in a mean way, like some of the other kids did, just in a curious way. One day during lunch, the teasing got really nasty, people calling me things like Kentucky Fried Bitch and stuff."

"Jesus. At twelve years old?"

"It's been a long time since you were in school, Detective. No offense. But you probably don't remember how awful girls can be."

"Fair enough. Go on."

"So, anyway, I was in the bathroom crying, and in walked the girl who was always staring at me in social studies. She asked me if my accent was real, and I said that it was, and she told me that she thought it was really cool and that I sounded like a country music star. It was a lie, but I really appreciated her saying it. She introduced herself and promised she would beat up anyone else who made fun of me, and that was kind of it. We became best friends." I smile at the memory.

"And when did you meet Jayne?"

"Not until the first time I was over at the Coopers' house, maybe two weeks after Sadie and I had started hanging out. I knew she was a twin, obviously, and I thought I'd maybe seen Jayne around the school, but she was in a bunch of advanced classes, and our paths had just never crossed. But I could tell Jayne didn't like me from the start."

"What makes you say that?"

I pause for a moment. I don't like to spend too much time

thinking about my first meeting with Jayne Cooper. It's easy to tell myself it's just because she was jealous, but it's more complicated than that.

"She, um, she told me something about Sadie. I remember that we were sitting in the kitchen, and Sadie had gone upstairs to get a sweatshirt or something, and I was trying to kind of chat with Jayne. Then Jayne just stopped the conversation and looked me right in the eyes, and she told me, 'My sister has a habit of collecting people like stray dogs. I'd be careful if I were you.'"

Detective Budd raises her perfect eyebrows. "She said that to you at twelve years old?"

"Once you talk to her, you'll realize it's kind of a normal sort of thing Jayne would say."

"Interesting. And how did you take that?"

"I took it as what it was. A threat."

"Hm."

I hate when people just say "hm" and nothing else. Shit or get off the pot, you know? I have no intention of following up on the "hm" until I realize that I still have zero power in this situation. Damn, Detective Budd is good. For a few minutes, I forgot that I was being interrogated.

"Fine," I say. "I'll bite. Why 'hm'?"

She cocks her head to one side and studies me carefully. "Do you suppose it's possible that Jayne was trying to warn you, not threaten you?"

Jayne Cooper, warn me? About her own sister? The idea is ridiculous, and I nearly laugh in Detective Budd's face. What would Jayne even have to warn me about back then? We were just kids. Sure, some shady shit has gone down since then, and Sadie hasn't always been the best friend. She hasn't always been as loyal as I've been. But it's different for her, dating Ben, being the golden girl. Sadie has dealt with levels of pressure that I'll never understand. It makes sense that sometimes she would lash out, or get angry at me, or ask me to take the blame for things.

It makes sense that I would have to deal with her shit to stay in the good graces of the Cooper family. For better or worse. Lately, it's been more and more for worse.

"Miss Stratton? I asked if you think it was possible that Jayne was trying to warn you. If there is anything about Sadie, anything that you know now as the person closest to her for years, that would help make sense of what Jayne said when you were kids."

"No, nothing. Sorry to disappoint you, Detective, but this is as simple as Jayne hating me because I took her place as Sadie's best friend."

Detective Budd seems satisfied, and she moves back to talking about the party last night. I'm relieved, even though this line of questioning is harder.

JAYNE

I'M NOT SURE how I'm supposed to react to the woman who just walked into this room. I know that her showing up made the local cops pretty angry, but that's about as far as my information goes. This is new for me. Usually, I'm one step ahead of everyone, especially the people who think they're running the show. But by the look of this woman, she's not just running the show—she is the show. And immediately, I admire her for that.

And anyway, there aren't enough women in law enforcement. It's not the career for me, but this lady can wear the hell out of a pantsuit without looking like a tragic accountant, and that's a feat worthy of celebration in and of itself. Sadie would have appreciated that observation—she and I always shared a very clear sense of style. Subtle differences, sure, but we always loved the same colors, the same kinds of dresses. It used to be something that was fun for us. But now I wonder if it's the reason she ended up dead instead of me.

"Jayne Cooper," the woman says, extending a hand across the table. "Detective Sloane Budd. I'm with the state. I'm so very sorry for the loss of your sister."

"Thanks," I reply quietly, shaking her hand. She isn't looking at me like I'm a drowning puppy in need of saving, which is a step up from Detective Hunt. My emotions made him uncomfortable, and he clearly didn't know what to do about that except to overreact in one direction or the other. In my experience, he's not unique in that. How is it that males never know what to do with emotions?

"I'm taking over from here," she continues, authority echoing in every word. "I know it's already been a long morning for you, and I promise to keep this as brief as possible."

"I'm here to help."

"Thank you. I understand you saw a disturbing photo that Mason Vreeland took in the darkroom at the school?"

I reach for my necklace. "Yeah," I say. "The police said they'd send someone to see if they could find it, but I don't know what Mason did with it after I freaked out and left. It was a picture of me, but I didn't know he'd taken it."

"How do you know it was you?"

I stare at her. What an asinine question. "I don't follow," I say simply.

"Is it possible it could have been your sister?"

"Absolutely not, Detective. Sadie and I might look identical to everyone else, but—and I don't mean this to sound rude—obviously, I know what I look like. I can tell the difference between myself and my sister, because I am not an idiot."

A smile tugs at one side of Detective Budd's mouth. "Touché," she says.

"And anyway, Mason and I were in photography club together. We spent time together, even though we weren't exactly friends or anything. And he asked me out once—after I turned him down, things got weird between us for a while, not because of anything I did, but because he just didn't seem to take the rejection well. I was as polite about it as I could be, but he seemed like the kind of guy who might have a short fuse. Super quiet until he exploded. You know the type?"

"I do."

"So, anyway, I'm positive it was a picture of me, and I recognized my necklace."

She's clearly interested in the necklace, so I take it off and offer it to her. "You can take a closer look."

She studies it. "It's very sweet," she says finally. "Sentimental value, I take it?"

I smile softly. "Now more than ever. It's not my typical style—I'm more of a fine jewelry girl, usually—but Sadie got this from a local vendor at the Christmas market last year. Hers and mine match."

Suddenly I realize I haven't asked a very important question. I'm almost afraid to, because once I know the answer, I can't unknow it.

"Um," I say, clearing my throat as tears rise up again. "I didn't ask Detective Hunt, but was Sadie . . . Does someone . . . ?"

Detective Budd knows what I'm getting at.

"Yes," she says, "Sadie had her necklace on last night. It's being tested by forensics right now, but you will get it back. I promise, I will make sure of it."

I nod, letting the tears start to fall again. "Thank you," I say.

Two halves of a broken heart, reunited. It's a twisted sort of ending, isn't it?

"Miss Cooper—Jayne, if I may. Detective Hunt said you prefer your first name. I'd like to learn more about what happened at the party itself last night."

"Sure. I didn't get there until late, but I'll tell you everything

I saw. Ben and Liz would probably be more helpful, if they're still here. Liz was with Sadie the whole night, and Ben—"

I don't have to say it. We all know how Ben Carrera was involved.

"I'm speaking to both of them, yes."

"Okay. Just . . . be careful."

"How do you mean?"

"With both of them, honestly. I'm sure you know by now that there was something going on between Liz and Ben, and I don't want to get either of them into any more trouble. I just . . ."

I pause, trying to choose my words carefully. There's no reason for Detective Budd to be too hard on them, but the longer I sit here, the more I get a bad feeling in the pit of my stomach that there is something bigger going on, and if I don't sound the alarm, I'll end up directly in the path of destruction.

"You just what?"

"I think Liz wanted a lot of what Sadie had, and I'm not sure how far she would've gone to get it. I'm not saying she had anything at all to do with what happened last night, but just . . . don't take what she says at face value."

"Would you care to be less cryptic? This is a murder investigation, Jayne, not gossip in the cafeteria. I am here to help you, and I can't do that if you don't shoot straight with me."

This is it, I guess. I came clean to Detective Hunt about Liz and Ben, and there's only one piece left to the whole thing that I haven't mentioned. I'm not sure why—maybe because I didn't think Hunt would be smart enough to understand why it was important.

"Sorry," I say. "This is all a lot. It's hard to know what might be important or not, or what might just be coincidence."

"There is no such thing as coincidence," Detective Budd says firmly. "Out with it, please."

Okay, then.

"Ask Liz about her necklace," I say slowly, watching as Detective Budd turns mine over in her hand subconsciously.

"What necklace?"

"That one you're holding," I begin. "It's mine. And Sadie had a matching one. But Liz had one too. It's so ridiculous, but she threw a huge tantrum when Sadie got these for us last Christmas. She was hurt that Sadie didn't choose her instead of me for the other half. Like I said, it's ridiculous. But Liz turned it into a whole thing, and my sister just couldn't stand it when anyone was upset with her. It was really important to her that she be on good terms with everyone all the time—we were always disagreeing on that, because how on earth is it possible to be liked by everyone? Anyway, she went out to the market the day after Christmas, when everything was at a fifty percent discount, obviously, and she got another one for Liz. Told her some story about how she really wanted to give the other half to her, but I was her sister and so she didn't want to upset me. Something about keeping the family peace."

"So there are three necklaces?"

"Yes. The one you're holding, the one Sadie was wearing, and the one Liz is wearing."

"Interesting." She's taking notes again.

"Is it? I wasn't sure if it mattered; I just thought it was something you should know."

"Was Miss Stratton wearing her necklace at the party last night?"

"Of course. She never takes it off."

"Never?"

"Never."

And I can tell in that moment, without Detective Budd saying anything else, that Liz is not wearing her necklace this morning.

"She doesn't have it, does she?" I ask.

"That's not a question I can answer for you, Jayne."

I shrug. "Fair enough. But hypothetically, if she's sitting in another godforsaken room in this station and she's not wearing a necklace just like that one, then if I were the police, I'd want to know what happened to it."

"I take your point."

And I know she does. Detective Budd isn't like the clowns who pass for police around here. She's smart enough to ask better questions and dig a layer deeper than the local guys ever would. Detective Hunt would probably have just shrugged me off and said that girls change their jewelry all the time. He wouldn't understand, but Detective Budd does.

Liz not having her necklace is significant somehow. It has to be.

"I'm really glad you're here," I say suddenly. "I don't know why you're involved or in charge now or whatever, but I feel a lot better about it. I just want you to know that."

She nods. "I appreciate your confidence, Jayne. I'll do my best to earn it. Now, let's get back to last night. Tell me what happened at Trevor McClain's."

"You ever have one of those nights where nothing goes the way you thought it would? I thought I'd be spending my Friday texting Evan and bingeing *Bridgerton*. But fate had other plans. And those other plans were me ending up at Trevor's party."

"Just don't be too stupid, okay?" It's not the best advice, but it's really all I can offer as Sadie and Liz walk out the door.

"We'll make good choices, Mom," Sadie replies dramatically. "Promise."

"Do you have your phone?"

Sadie double-checks her bag and nods.

"Come on, let's get going," Liz says. She's bouncing on the balls of her feet like she's about to sprint to Trevor's if they don't leave the

house this very second. I wonder why she's so anxious to get there. She's been flirting a little bit with this guy Justin in our class, but he's definitely not the kind of guy I'd be in a rush to go meet in a cornfield.

Then again, there isn't any guy I'd be in a rush to go meet in a cornfield.

I wave them off and breathe a sigh of relief when the door shuts behind them. Finally, I have the house to myself. I'm looking forward to a quiet night in.

Evan's name lights up my screen as I'm changing into my sweats. I can't help but smile. He might have ditched me for the weekend, but at least it left the night open for a different kind of fun. I tell him the game is on. I don't have to say anything else. Evan already knows what I mean. I'm just about to collapse on the couch a few minutes later when a text from my mom comes in.

On our way home. Dad forgot his meds.

Well, this was definitely not part of my plan.

It's a little past nine p.m. I check the recipients—me and Sadie. I quickly send back a thumbs-up, hoping that will stop my sister from responding with anything that she thinks seems normal but would not be remotely close to the response a sober person would have. Sadie is like that, the sort of drunk girl who thinks she still seems sober.

My first thought is that this is not going to end well. Sadie is going to end up in deep trouble. My second thought is that I'm going to have to scrap my other plans for a quiet night in.

I text Sadie and ask her what time they're going to be home. It's a ridiculous question, because they only just got to Trevor's an hour ago. When I don't get a response from her, I try texting Liz. Still nothing.

Based on the time, my parents are definitely already at the lake, and they've probably been there for a few hours. It'll be at least three hours until they're home, but with Sadie and Liz both not responding, it's becoming clear pretty quickly that I'm going to have to go to Trevor's to get them. I text Evan about how my plans for the night have been so rudely interrupted, and he gives me some ridiculous platitude about joining them if you can't beat 'em.

I stare at Evan's words. He's not entirely wrong . . . If I have to haul myself to Trevor McClain's cornfield, I can at least have a little bit of fun with it. That's why I decide to put on an outfit like the one Sadie was wearing when she left—a black crop top and loose low-rise jeans. We do this sometimes, Sadie and I. Dress alike just to mess with people. Hopefully, she won't mind if I do it tonight. And to be honest, I've made such a big deal about not having any interest in parties like this one that if I get confused for Sadie while I'm there, it will actually help save my reputation a little bit. And if I'm sober and not making an idiot out of myself, it might help save Sadie's reputation a little bit too.

"What game were you referring to in your text to Evan Garfield?"

"It's just something we say to each other," I explain, wondering why that's the thing she's choosing to focus on from my story. And why I even mentioned it.

"Okay, and so the matching outfits . . . that's why you and Sadie were dressed exactly alike?"

"Yes. It seems so silly now, especially because—" I feel the tears start to flow again, but I make myself say it. "Because that might be the reason she's dead."

"You had no way of knowing what Mason Vreeland was planning."

"Do you think he was? Planning it, I mean? Like, it was premeditated?"

"We don't know. That could be true, but it could also be true that Sadie rejected him or did something else that upset him, and he lashed out."

"I'm not sure which is worse."

"Either way, the result is the same."

My face must change as soon as she says those words, because Detective Budd quickly adds on, "I'm sorry, Jayne. I don't mean to be harsh."

"It's all right," I reply. "I always appreciate people who tell the truth, no matter the circumstances. It's amazing how many little lies people tell every single day. I prefer to live as honestly as I can, and I'm drawn to people who live that way too."

"Is your friend Evan one of those people?"

I smile in spite of myself. "Absolutely."

* * *

By the time I get to Trevor's, I still haven't heard a word from Sadie or Liz. Reception isn't the best this far outside of town, but as much as I'd like to chalk it up to spotty service, I know the truth is that they're both wasted, and at this point, Sadie has probably had some kind of fight with Ben and thrown her phone at him. I know my sister, and I know her relationship with Ben. It isn't a mystery that her fuse with him has gotten shorter ever since what happened with Liz last year. He's basically walking on eggshells, and the slightest thing—being late for a date, not meeting her outside her English class so they can walk to lunch together, promising to wear one shirt to a party and then showing up in a different one—can light the match these days.

I know I shouldn't be so happy about the current state of their relationship, but I've always said that Sadie can be so much more than just Mrs. Carrera, no matter how much she doodles in notebooks or types it into the Notes section of her phone (don't get me started on the photos she's saving in an album she calls "Future Wedding"). If the situation with Liz and Sadie's inability to truly, deeply forgive Ben for it is the thing that ultimately pushes them apart . . . I don't know. I'd be there for Sadie, of course, but I would also be cheering louder than anyone when she finally realized everything with Ben was just a high school dalliance.

As luck would have it, the first person I make eye contact with when I walk through the door is Mason Vreeland. He's talking to a group of guys from school, but I don't know any of their names.

Mostly art kids, I think, and I once again find myself surprised that he actually came to this party. When our eyes meet, I'm not sure what to do with myself. The first instinct I have is that I desperately need a drink, but the warm beer in kegs and cheap gas-station vodka are a far cry from what I would normally stomach.

Still, with Evan's text echoing in my head—if you can't beat 'em, join 'em—I head for the nearest massive black trash can full of a mystery mixed drink and dunk a plastic red Solo cup into it. I take one sip and nearly gag. Absolutely not.

"You can't run away forever, you know." Mason has appeared next to me, brushing his dark brown hair away from his eyes. He has brown eyes, and they have a habit of looking as though they're piercing into your soul. It would be unnerving under normal circumstances to be this close to him, but after what I saw in the photography lab, I feel even more like a cornered animal. It's not a feeling I enjoy.

"Back off, Mason. I have nothing to say to you."

I say it more to get out of the conversation, but when I move away, Mason puts a hand on my shoulder.

"Hold on," he says. His tone has completely changed. "Jayne? Is that you?"

For a moment, I think he's kidding me, but then I realize it's a serious question. And of course it is. I'm dressed like Sadie, and no one expects me to show up at this kind of thing. Of course he thought I was my sister.

"Guilty," I say. "But if anyone asks, I'm not even here."

"Not a word. Cross my heart and hope to die. But do me a favor. If you see your sister around here, tell her that our conversation isn't over."

"So you interacted with Mason Vreeland at Trevor's?"

"Yeah. Like I said, he thought I was Sadie, but he . . . obviously he knew I was there after that. The interaction felt so creepy. And it was strange, how he started the conversation—saying, 'You can't run away forever.' Telling me that his conversation with Sadie wasn't over."

"Did you ask him what he meant or confront him about the picture in the photography lab?"

"No. I thought about it, but I didn't see the point. He had obviously been drinking—"

"What makes you say 'obviously'?"

"Well, he had a drink in his hand. And he smelled like alcohol. It didn't take a rocket scientist to figure that out. And there was just something about seeing him there. I had always thought Mason didn't care about what other people thought of him, that he was above it. I thought he saw through all the petty high school nonsense like I do. But I think maybe he did care. Seeing him last night proved that to me. He was trying, in his own way, to fit in with the rest of them."

"And do you have any idea what he might have meant about his conversation with Sadie?"

I take a deep breath.

"I think they were fighting about me," I say finally. "I think Mason might have been harassing my sister last night, following her around and trying to get her to agree to talk to me for him, explain something about the photo, maybe? Like I said, he asked me out a while back and just got very strange about it when I said no."

"Isn't it possible that he had transferred his affections to Sadie?"

"What?"

"You rejected him; he knew he had no shot. Maybe he was interested in Sadie."

"No, that's not it." I see the way the detective is looking at me. I need her to understand. To believe me. "Everyone knew Sadie was with Ben. Mason never would've had a chance against Ben, and he knew it. Besides, I could tell he was still into me. You know how you just know?"

She nods. She's a pretty woman; she knows what I mean.

"My sister is dead because of me. I'm sure of it."

LIZ

IT'S ONE OF *those nights that just feels like it's going to end in disaster. Sadie is drinking way more than she usually does, and even though I'm trying to maintain control of the situation by pouring watered-down drinks for her to make sure she's not drinking straight vodka, I know I'm not the only one pouring.*

Ben has his arm around her in the corner like she's a piece of luggage. You know the way guys can do that—just sort of casually tossing an arm over a girl, not even around her. It's possession, not love, and I would know because I've been on the receiving end of it more times than I can count. Usually, the guy is a lot older. Usually, there's something I want badly enough that I'll tolerate his bullshit so I can get it.

But tonight, seeing Ben and Sadie together just makes me sad. It's been complicated ever since what happened last year, and it's not that I'm sad because I wish it were me instead of her with Ben. It's just . . . sad. I feel like I can see their entire lives playing out in front of my eyes, and I wish Sadie could see it too and run as far away in the other direction as she can.

Although, as I constantly try to remind myself when it comes to the Coopers—not my life, not my problem. My mom used to have a phrase that went something like that. She would say, "Not my circus, not my monkeys," which always made me laugh when I was little. I'd ask her where the monkeys were, and she would inevitably say, "I see one right in front of me!" and start tickling me.

I smile in spite of myself, even in the middle of the drunken chaos of Trevor's. I probably don't think about my mom as often as I should. (I don't know how often you're supposed to think about a dead parent. Does it depend on how old you were when they died? What kind of relationship you had with them? Whether or not they unintentionally saddled you with a religious freak of a stepfather?)

The smile doesn't stay on my face for long, though, because at about ten p.m., Jayne Cooper walks through the door. I have to do a double take, because for a second, I think she's Sadie and that she just somehow got outside to the bonfire and is coming back inside.

Jayne is dressed in the exact same outfit as Sadie. My brain can't quite make sense of it in the moment, but then I realize: If Jayne is here, I can only assume something has gone horribly wrong. Are Steven and Carly here too somehow? Or are they coming back early? Did Jayne just suddenly, against every piece of her character I've ever understood, decide that she really wanted to drink shitty beer in a field with the rest of us commoners? And dress like her sister to do it?

I turn around to the corner previously occupied by Ben and Sadie to warn Sadie that her sister is here and to hopefully try to get her even vaguely, partially more sober than she is now. But she and Ben are both gone.

"Just my luck," I mutter to myself. Figuring it's better to talk to Jayne myself instead of waiting for her to track down Sadie, I make my way over to her.

The house is so packed that Jayne has barely had the chance to move more than two feet from the front door, and I grab another cup of beer from one of the tables nearby on my way to her as a peace offering. And also because I figure it'll piss her off to even be handed something so beneath her.

"Jayne," I say. "To what do we owe the . . . pleasure . . . of your company?"

She eyes me up with a level of distaste that she usually has the good sense to hide in front of Sadie.

* * *

"Let's pause here. You saw Jayne walk through the door at Trevor McClain's house?"

"Yeah."

"And would you say that you were the very first person to talk to her at the party? That she didn't even have the time to speak with anyone else before you got over to her?"

I give Detective Budd a look that I hope conveys how completely useless this line of questioning is, but she's been nice enough so far, and I figure it can't hurt to humor her.

"Right," I reply. "Jayne walked through the door around ten—I remember because Trevor's parties have this 'ten for ten' kind of thing that the guys do."

"God help me for asking, but what is 'ten for ten'?"

"Trevor rounds up ten guys in the first hour or so of the night, and then at ten o'clock, the so-called chosen ones have to do ten shots. They had just finished up, and that's how I know what time Jayne showed up."

"Yikes."

I shrug. "Like I said before, been a while since you've been in school, huh?"

"Watch it, Miss Stratton," Detective Budd replies, but I can tell she's at least a little bit amused. But as I watch her face, it transforms almost imperceptibly from amusement to suspicion.

I know that look well. It's one of Levi's favorites when he's looking at me.

"You're sure, then, that it was ten p.m., and that Jayne didn't speak to anyone else before you came up and offered her a drink? What about immediately after that?"

"After that? We were going to go looking for Sadie together. She told me that Steven and Carly were on their way home, which was basically a four-alarm emergency. I wanted to ask her about the shit I'd seen her taking out of her dad's bag, but I figured that was a question for Saturday morning, not Friday night."

Detective Budd is furiously taking notes, and it's making me feel increasingly insecure. This is all basic stuff; why is she writing like her life depends on it or something?

"Did you have a text from Jayne telling you that her parents were coming home and asking when you and Sadie would be back?"

"What? No." I shake my head. "Jayne and I are not exactly texting buddies. I assume she texted Sadie, but, no, she never texted me." I pause. "Why? Did she say she did?"

Detective Budd doesn't answer me.

"Okay, what's going on?" I say finally. "I'm just telling you the timeline. I don't understand why you're being so obsessive right now."

She takes a break from staring at her notebook and looks

up at me. "First of all, Miss Stratton, the obsessiveness you're referring to is called doing my job. Second of all, you may as well know, in case it changes anything you're telling me, that the reason I'm taking such detailed notes right now about your account of the evening is because—and I'm going to shoot straight with you here, because you deserve that—what you're telling me right now does not match up with what Jayne Cooper is telling me."

My heart drops in my chest like a block of cement. I can feel my pulse racing. Sweat starting to form on my temples. Shit. Shit, shit, shit. This is the reaction of someone who is guilty of something—I've seen enough true crime shows to know that. But I'm not guilty. Not like that. What the hell is going on here?

"I can see that's news to you," Detective Budd says, eyeing me carefully.

"Um." I take a deep breath, trying to steady myself. "Yeah. Yeah, that is news to me."

"Now that you're aware, is there anything else you'd like to tell me about what happened when Jayne showed up? Anything that you might be remembering differently now?"

I wish I could say yes. I should say yes. Detective Sloane Budd's eyes, so open and frank when she first came into this room with my bag of McDonald's, are now impossible to read. And I know why. I've just gone from a witness to be pitied to a suspect to be interrogated.

Fuck.

"Did something happen to your necklace?" Detective Budd asks me suddenly.

My hand instinctively flies up to my neck, and I remember it's not there.

Jayne must have told her about our necklaces. I wonder if she told her BS story that Sadie gave it to her first.

"Miss Stratton?"

"Oh, I . . ." I can barely get the words out. I start crying—like, ugly crying. Detective Budd must think I'm losing it.

"I lost it somehow last night," I say through my tears. "I don't know what happened to it. I literally never take it off, except to shower. I wear it everywhere. And I lost it last night, of all nights. I'm such a shitty best friend. Such an idiot. It's the most important thing Sadie ever gave me, and I managed to lose it . . . on the same night I lost her."

Detective Budd now looks at me with such pity that it just makes me cry harder.

JAYNE

AFTER MY INTERACTION *with Mason, the only thing I want to do is find Sadie. Trevor's house is absolutely packed with people, and it's impossible to tell where she might be. There's a massive bonfire outside near the old barn that I caught sight of when I first got here, and I figure that might be as good a place as any to start. A quick scan of the room tells me that she isn't here, although it's just as likely that she's upstairs with Ben somewhere. I guess they could also be screaming at each other in the cornfield right now. To-may-to, to-mah-to. It's a fine line with those two, although, to be honest, Ben is the emotional one, really. Everyone thinks it's Sadie, but she's more logical than people give her credit for. That's probably one of the reasons she's still with Ben—logic. Good future, good family (except for the whole murder thing with Ben's uncle), good money.*

Whenever I think about the two of them, it reminds me of something that Meg Ryan's character says in When Harry Met Sally*. She and Billy Crystal's character are talking about whether or not Ilsa really wanted to stay with Rick at the end of* Casablanca*, which is one of my favorite old movies. Anyway, Meg's character basically argues that Ilsa would rather go with Victor Laszlo and be first lady of wherever than stay in Casablanca with a guy who owns a bar. And that's what I think about when it comes to Sadie and Ben—that Sadie would rather be first lady of wherever than stuck in Casablanca with a guy who owns a bar. Happiness is not a factor. Practicality is, even if Sadie herself hasn't realized it yet.*

I'm a practical girl too. I just happen to have very different ambitions than my sister and a very different set of ends that justify the means.

Right now, though, my only end involves finding Sadie and getting her home before my parents show up. It sounds simple, but it's anything but—especially since I've set the ambitious goal of not just getting Sadie home but Liz too, if I can find her, and preferably getting them both upstairs and asleep in Sadie's room within the next hour or so. The last thing any of us needs is for them to be awake and obviously drunk when Steven and Carly show up. All I need to see is the text from my mom to know that she is not happy about having to come back and probably even more angry at my dad for somehow forgetting the one thing they need before they travel anywhere.

"Would you consider your father a forgetful man? Has he ever forgotten his medication before?"

I pause for a moment, pulling myself out of the scene from last night and back to the present moment before I take a detour into memories of family vacations. Steven Cooper is a lot of things, but forgetful isn't necessarily one of them. Unless, of course, he's distracted.

"It's happened once or twice," I say finally. "But normally he's able to just call someone and have his medication ready to pick up at the local pharmacy. I think the only reason they decided to come home is because there weren't any drugstores open, and it was easier to just drive back."

Detective Sloane Budd is paying close attention to everything I'm telling her, and I appreciate that. It's important to feel like someone is listening—actually listening, not just putting on a show of it like some of these local detectives. I try to give them the benefit of the doubt. I can't imagine working around here is the best way to hone your policing skills or get paid a living wage. But Detective Budd is here because she is personally invested in this case. I get the sense that somehow she has something at stake here. And while I don't entirely understand what or why, I am more than willing to cooperate.

"By the way," she says, almost casually, "there seem to be some inconsistencies with what you and Liz Stratton are saying about the party."

"What kind of inconsistencies?"

"Just . . . timing. What happened after you showed up. Who you first spoke to, for example."

I rub my face and shake my head. How is it that Sadie is gone and Liz is still messing with this family?

"Look," I say, not bothering to hide the exhaustion in my voice. "I don't know what Liz told you, and to be frank, I don't need to know. She was absolutely plastered last night."

"She said—"

"Let me guess. She said that she doesn't drink anymore, right? Or some other cop told you that she said that? I don't mean to be disrespectful, Detective Budd, but that is a flat-out lie, and if you believe it, then you're doing yourself a disservice in my sister's case. What I'm telling you is the truth. I showed up at the party, got cornered by Mason Vreeland when I attempted to get myself something that could only vaguely be considered to resemble a drink, and I got out of that situation as fast as I could. You can check my texts—I told Evan about it as soon as it happened."

"Did you see Miss Stratton when you came into the room?"

I pause, racking my brain.

"No," I say finally. "If I'd seen her when I first came in, I would have asked her where Sadie was and tried to corral both of them into the car. I didn't see her until later in the night, out by the bonfire. And like I said, she was wasted at that point. I'm not trying to get her into trouble; I'm sure she's doing her best to fill in the blanks of last night. She must feel as awful as I do about everything that happened. She's probably just . . . I don't know, trying to imagine what might have happened and calling that the truth."

"Interesting theory."

I shrug. "It's more than a theory, Detective. Liz has done this in the past. Blacked out and then tried to fill in the blanks with whatever version of the story she thought would work best for her audience. I don't mean to sound harsh or judgmental, but I just can't let this stand. My sister is dead, and I don't care if Liz wishes she remembered what happened last night." My eyes are starting to well up again—they keep doing that anytime I actually have to utter the words about Sadie's death—and I let the tears go. "She doesn't remember, and nothing is going to change that. It's her cross to bear, and I hurt for her, I really do, because that must be hard. The guilt must be hard. But I'm not going to sit here and let her tell you lies about what happened last night just to soothe her conscience. It's wrong."

"I'll note that you disagree with her version of events."

"Vehemently disagree," I reply.

"Duly noted. Thank you for your candor, Jayne."

"Well, I'm under oath, aren't I?"

"Not quite. This isn't a trial. But in a manner of speaking, let's say so."

"Well, then, you should know, Detective, that Sadie and I always made pinky promises to each other when . . . when we were both here. It may sound immature, but it was our thing. A twin thing. And I'll give you the same thing that I gave her—my promise."

"Thank you, Jayne. So, if you didn't see Miss Stratton when you first came in, what happened after you had the interaction with Mason Vreeland?"

I tuck my phone away after a quick back-and-forth with Evan. I'm looking forward to updating him as soon as this whole night shakes out. He's already been talking to me about his big plans for a spring break group vacation before we all go off to college next year. No details yet, but I can't wait to get out of here and escape to wherever Evan considers "somewhere classy, with classy people." I haven't met any of Evan's other friends, and he hasn't really met anyone here either, aside from my family, Ben, and Liz. That's the thing about a long-distance friendship. Something I appreciate about it, actually. It allows me to curate myself a little bit more, almost like dress rehearsal for getting out of this town and building a new life for myself in college.

But right now, I am anywhere but somewhere classy. I fight my way through the crowd of people in Trevor's house and take a deep breath when I finally make it out the back door and the cold autumn air hits my lungs. How on earth do people even breathe here?

The bonfire is already blazing, and I faintly wonder how Trevor pulls off things like this without burning his parents' field to the ground. Then again, Trevor McClain is the kind of guy who is endlessly creative when it comes to putting together a party. Even though I've never been to one of them, they're legendary for a reason.

"Do you know if Mason Vreeland frequently went to parties at Trevor's house?" Detective Budd interrupts.

"I couldn't possibly tell you," I reply. "Like I just said, last night was the first time I'd ever been to one of Trevor's parties myself. Liz would know."

"Wouldn't Trevor McClain be the best person for me to ask?"

I shrug. "Honestly, probably not. There must have been a hundred people there last night, maybe more, and I can't imagine it's ever any different. Trevor probably has no idea who actually shows up."

"Fair enough. Let me switch topics for a moment—at what point in the night did you first see Ben Carrera?"

At the mention of Ben's name, my hackles go up. I can't help it.

"He's telling you the truth," I say simply. "About what happened last night."

"That's not the question I asked, Jayne."

"I know, but it's where all this is leading. Did I see Ben; if so, when; was he drunk; and was there anything else to note about his situation with Sadie or Mason? I've seen enough old detective movies to know this song and dance, Detective Budd. I'm simply trying to streamline this process for both of us."

For a moment, I think Detective Budd is about to go along with me, and we can just wind down this entire unfortunate situation. I desperately want to go home. I need to see my parents. I need to lie down in my own bed. I need to come to terms with my new future. I need to talk to Evan.

"I'm sorry, Jayne, but we are still going to have to go through the whole—how did you put it?—song and dance. Hazard of the trade, I'm afraid, no matter how much you or anyone else might like to skip ahead to the part where this is resolved in a neat and tidy way."

"My sister was stabbed to death, Detective. I don't think there's any such thing as a 'neat and tidy' resolution. I'm not a fool."

"I never said you were."

In this moment, I almost miss the local detective who was bringing me terrible cups of tea and doing his best to relate to the feelings of a teenage girl. I liked Detective Sloane Budd when she first came into the room, but I'm starting to get more than a little tired of the third degree and play-by-play of last night. I have zero desire to relive the events of the past twenty-four hours and even less of a desire to get backed into a corner that ends with me telling her something that will get Ben in even more trouble than he's in now.

Because the good news for Ben Carrera is that, as long as the trouble isn't too bad, his father can get him out of it. I know that for a fact. And in this particular case, murdering a guy from school who just killed his girlfriend qualifies to me as something that might be bad but isn't too bad. There's really no reason for the detective to start looking under rocks in search of something more. This story is what it is, and none of us can change it.

BEN

MY FATHER ARRIVED about five minutes after I was dragged back into the interrogation room by the lady detective whose name I've already forgotten. And about one minute after that, he was sitting down next to me with cups of coffee for both of us.

"You look like hell, son," he says, not even a trace of affection in his voice. "Jesus, what have you gotten yourself into?"

That's the thing about Donovan Carrera. Anyone who sees him here will see a father deeply concerned about his son. Bringing him coffee, sitting in the room with him to offer moral support and keep the cops from trying anything shady. But I know my dad, and the real reason he's here is because all this looks pretty damn bad for his reputation. And what's bad for his reputation is bad for his business. My father has very little patience for anything that is bad for business. He didn't build the Carrera name up from nothing—less than nothing, honestly—for it to be torn down by his only child.

In fact, I imagine he's already turning over in his mind the ways that Sadie's murder will end up helping Steven Cooper come out on top this year. The two are working on a major development together, but they both still seem to be keeping score. Still trying to one-up each other like they did back in high school. The thing is, though, my dad should be smarter than that. He's a winner, and winners operate under the constant belief that the game is already won.

"Gentlemen, thank you for joining me." The lady detective sweeps into the room and shuts the door behind her with force. She's the kind of woman who was probably smoking hot fifteen years ago, and she's still not bad now, although now that I can see her up close and in bright light, I realize that this line of work clearly isn't doing her any favors.

I expect my father to speak first, and I'm anticipating that he's about to rail against this woman for keeping me held hostage here and demand to know why the state is involved. I expect him to bring every inch of his six-foot-four, former-football-player body into the conversation and tower over this petite woman like the mountain of stone he is.

That's what I expect. But that isn't what happens.

"Sloane Budd," he says simply, quietly. "I'll be damned."

The lady detective—Detective Budd, or whatever—smiles. "Not while I have anything to say about it," she replies. "It's good to see you, though, Donovan. I'm sorry about the circumstances."

They shake hands, and my father clasps her hand with both of his. "You and me both," he replies. "At least somebody with a brain stepped in around here. I appreciate the favor."

Detective Budd shrugs. "I figured the ask came from you once I got the details of the case. It's the least I can do. And, hey, I heard you're doing well for yourself these days. Must be, to call in a favor like this. I'm glad for you. It's hard-earned, and you deserve it."

I've been trying to keep my calm during this baffling interaction, but I can't anymore.

"Can one of you please tell me what the hell is going on?" I ask finally. "Dad, you know this woman?"

"Benjamin." My father always insists on calling me Benjamin. It never ceases to annoy me. "This is Detective Sloane Budd. She was on the local beat here when your Uncle Christopher was killed. She's the only one who believed I didn't do it. I owe the entire life I've built for you and your mother to her. She was a damn persistent rookie, no matter how many higher-ups she pissed off with her stubborn streak."

There is a look in my father's eyes that I've honestly never seen before, and it takes me a moment to realize what it is. Admiration. He actually admires and respects this woman. Hell, he's happy she's here.

He asked her to be here.

"Um." I'm not sure what to say to that. "Right. Well . . . um . . . cool."

She nods in my general direction without taking her eyes off my father.

"We never did nail the guy who really did it, though," she says, shaking her head. "I'm sorry about that, Donovan."

"Not your fault. You were a rookie—what were you supposed to do when they closed the investigation? Even if you'd threatened to quit, it wouldn't have made a difference."

"True. The captain just transferred me instead, anyway. Turned out to be the best thing that could have happened to me."

My father nods approvingly. "I can see that. And I put it behind me, so here we both are. And anyway, we aren't here to talk about the past. We're here to talk about the very unfortunate situation we're dealing with at present."

My dad's face looks very grim at the mention of "the very unfortunate situation."

"We are. And thank you for being here in person. Given the sensitive nature of the incident and your son's involvement, I thought it would be best to have a parent present while I continue the questioning."

"It's kind of you to extend the courtesy."

"You deserve the courtesy, Don."

Okay, what the hell is going on here? My father flips out if anyone dares to call him Don. It's the ultimate insult, and yet when this bitch does it, he smiles like it's a beloved nickname? The only thing I can think is that he's putting her on, trying to build back up to whatever kind of rapport they had back when my uncle was killed. He was clearly able to manipulate her back then, and if he called in a favor to get her here now, I can only imagine he has the same plan this time around. He probably just needs some bleeding heart to agree that this whole thing is a tragic mess and then sweep it under the rug where it belongs. I guess I just need to trust that he knows what he's doing.

I briefly wonder if he slept with this woman—it would have been before he and my mom were married, although only barely, and I can see how they might have been each other's type twenty years ago.

But speculating about my father's love life before my existence isn't particularly helpful. I can feel myself starting to spin out again, and I locate the small piece of green tape on the floor from before. Obviously, the smudge on the coffee cup isn't here anymore, but there is the tape.

Green tape.

Okay.

I am here.

I stare at my dad, trying to figure out what he's playing at.

Because here's the thing. My dad killed my Uncle Chris. I'm almost positive. I don't know exactly what went down and if there was more to it than that girl or whatever, but I know my dad, and it sounds like my uncle screwed him over somehow. I know my dad is not someone to just take that. Even when it's family . . . maybe especially when it's family.

It's weird, knowing your dad is a murderer. But if I'm being honest, I've always respected that about him. Knowing that he did whatever it took. Because I did whatever it took too last night. I did what had to be done. Just like him.

I can even admire the fact that he has this Sloane woman fooled into believing that he had nothing to do with it. After all, that's probably what got him off. All he needed was one stupid cop to fall for the story he was selling and *boom*. Done deal. It's brilliant, really.

And I can only assume the main reason he showed up here is because he's about to talk us out of this room and talk me out of prison time for what I did. He's got to understand, probably better than anyone. I'll admit it; in the few moments they've left me alone in here, I've built up this idea of what would happen when my father showed up. In my imagination, he shows up swearing and brandishing every relationship he's got at every level of government in the whole state. Hell, maybe even in the whole country. And he tells me that I did what I had to do, which is what makes a man a real man. A real leader. And the two of us get the hell out of here in his Range Rover, and we just keep on driving until we're far outside the town limits.

Then he takes a bottle of whisky out of the back seat, and we each take a swig while he tells me that I finally made him proud. That I'm finally a leader, and I did what I had to do, just like he did. That's how he knows I'm ready to take over the family business. Not after college, not ten years from now, but right now. Today.

I've spun this idea around my brain so many times that I can practically taste the whisky. I'm already gone in my head, and my father and I are partners in crime.

I haven't been paying attention to what they've been talking about, but when I tune back in, I realize the detective lady is filling him in on what happened last night. How I strangled Mason with my bare hands.

My dad looks . . . horrified? Disgusted? A little queasy?

What he doesn't look is proud. No slap on the back. No *Way to go, son; that bastard deserved it.*

My dad kind of looks like he might cry.

What the actual fuck is happening right now?

"So, as horrific as it all is, it does seem like a very clear-cut case of self-defense," Detective Budd is saying. It's almost like she's trying to console my dad. "I just need to ask Ben a few more questions. I'm honestly not foreseeing any issues, Don. Jayne Cooper's story matches Ben's."

My father turns to me and puts a hand on my shoulder.

"Benjamin, you're in good hands with Detective Budd. Just be honest with her. Explain what happened, exactly how it happened."

I'm confused.

"What do you mean?" I ask. "Aren't you staying in here? Didn't you come here to get me so we could just be done with all this?"

"Not quite yet. I'm sorry, Benjamin, but you need to go through this process, the same way I did. A boy is dead because of you, son. We know it was justified, but you need to explain everything that happened. The truth will win out, as long as the local assholes aren't the ones in charge. You have nothing to hide, so just be honest with Detective Budd and let the chips fall where they may."

Let the chips fall where they may? What is happening right now? The whole reason I wasn't worried—the whole reason I knew that I'd be okay, no matter what I did last night—was because I'm Ben Carrera. I don't have to let the chips fall where they may; I just have to stand back and let the chips fall where my father puts them.

The knot that has been slowly forming in my stomach intensifies. I try to focus on the green tape on the floor. To stay in the moment. It's not working.

In less than five minutes, the presence of Sloane Budd has torn apart every single thing I thought I knew about my father. I thought we were the same, me and my dad, even though he might think we're different. Last night proved that we were the same. That I could be as much of a man as he was and do what needed to be done.

But I was wrong. Everything I thought I knew about Donovan Carrera was a lie.

What am I supposed to do now?

"You don't need to look so frightened, Mr. Carrera," Detective Budd says as my dad leaves the room, giving me a smile that is meant to be sympathetic but just makes my blood boil.

"I'm not frightened," I reply, aware of how angry I sound. But honestly, I am angry. So why should I try to hide it?

"All right, then. Well, whatever you're feeling, it's normal. Rage, anger, sadness, horror . . . any and all those feelings are okay."

"If I wanted to talk about my feelings, I would talk to a goddamn therapist."

"Take a deep breath, Mr. Carrera. I am not trying to be combative with you, and my hope is that you won't try to be combative with me, either. This situation is awful enough as it is. I'm just trying to understand your side of the story."

My side of the story. Sure. Isn't that what the last couple guys who were in here said they were trying to do? Am I stuck in a time loop?

"Mr. Carrera." She's trying to be gentle with me, and I hate when women do that. Talk to you like you're a child who somehow can't comprehend what they're saying or like you're one step away from a complete meltdown. Sadie used to talk to me like that sometimes. She used to do a lot of things that were infuriating. As it turns out, I didn't know about the worst of them until a week ago.

That's when I found out Sadie was cheating on me. That's when I found out that even though she made such a big deal about her virginity—saying she wanted to wait until after graduation and all that other bullshit—she'd already given it away to some other guy. She was ready to do it; she just hadn't wanted to do it with me.

Bitch.

She never would have even told me herself. In fact, she never *did* tell me herself. I heard about it from someone else. From the person closer to her than anyone in the world. The person who knew exactly how much it would hurt me after I spent so much time trying to make up for what I did with Liz that night. The person who thought I deserved to know and also thought that I deserved to decide what I wanted to do about it.

The thing is, what happened between me and Liz didn't mean anything. When your girlfriend flat-out refuses to sleep with you, and then her best friend starts texting you, and saying how hot you are, and then practically throws herself at you at a party when your girlfriend isn't around . . . what's a guy supposed to do? I'm not made of stone. Liz was begging me to screw her that night. She didn't have to say it out loud for me to know. We'd been texting back and forth since spring break, and it was obvious she wanted me. It's not like I was even her first or anything. At the party that night . . . Well, like I said, I'm not made of stone.

It would have been our little secret, mine and Liz's, if she'd even remembered it at all. But it was just my luck that Jayne happened to be there with her friend Evan. She's the one who walked in on us, and I knew she wasn't going to keep it to herself. She's the kind of girl who knows exactly how to use the information she has to get what she wants. If my father is to be believed, she gets that from Steven Cooper, who has more than a few skeletons in his closet. The apple doesn't fall far from the tree, you know?

"Mr. Carrera." Detective Budd's voice is no longer sweet.

Now she just sounds annoyed. "Do we need to get your father back in here to get you to start talking again? I'd prefer to keep whatever you have to say between us, and I imagine you do too. But if this can't happen without him—"

"Of course it can happen without him," I reply sharply. "I'm not a child."

Satisfied that she's at least gotten some kind of answer out of me, Detective Budd seems to relax. "Okay, then," she says. "Now that we've got the lines of communication open again, why don't you tell me what happened last night, starting with what brought you out to the barn where you discovered Sadie and Mason Vreeland."

"Sure." I rub my hands through my hair, very aware of the fact that I never got that shower I was so desperately hoping for.

"I was kind of on high alert last night," I start off.

"Why was that?"

"Honestly, it didn't start out that way. Me and Sadie met up at Trevor's, and we were having a great time. I was pouring her drinks, and Liz might have been too. Liz was just kind of around, you know? Flirting with some other guys there, doing her thing."

"Did it bother you at all to see Liz flirting with other guys?"

"What? No. What kind of a stupid question is that?"

"I'm aware that the two of you still text now and then. I'm

just wondering if there was anything else going on last night that would have made you feel upset."

"No." My voice is getting louder. "Absolutely not. That's the most idiotic thing I've ever heard."

"And yet you seem pretty upset right now just by me bringing it up."

"I'm upset because I was passed off from local detectives who actually understand this town and this case to some bitch from the state who doesn't seem to know back from front."

As soon as I say it, I realize I've made a terrible mistake. This is not the woman to mess with, and I basically just verbally punched her in the face.

"Well, Mr. Carrera," she says after a moment of silence. Her voice is calm. "You may think I'm just . . . what was it? Some bitch from the state? And that may be true; I've been called worse in my day. But I am the bitch who is now in charge of this case, and you can be in some very serious trouble if you don't cooperate right now. Frankly, you can be in serious trouble even if you *do* cooperate right now. But losing your temper with me, regardless of how stressful the current circumstances are, is not going to help your case. If anything, it will just make things worse for you, a fact that I'm sure you can understand. Now, can you be civil with me and answer my questions, or do we need to handcuff you and try this again in a jail cell? And before you answer, I'd like you to remember that only one of those options would be acceptable to your father."

She's right. I know she's right. But the thing that really gets me is the idea that my father had the power to walk in here and stop this, and instead, he threw me to the wolves.

I wonder if I ought to demand that he come back in here—this bitch was being a lot nicer to him than she is to me—but I dismiss the idea as quickly as it comes to me. All that would prove is that I don't know how to handle myself. That I don't know how to lead, and I still need my father to come in here and get me out of the mess I made. Not that I made it all by myself . . .

I got this. I just have to get this back on track.

"I apologize," I say, trying to sound like I mean it at least a little bit. "I'm very sorry, Detective Budd. That wasn't appropriate. Obviously, I mean no disrespect to you. Especially knowing how highly my father thinks of you and everything you did for him after what happened to Uncle Chris. I'm just so upset about last night. It's really hard to get my head on straight, and my nerves are fried. I'm not reacting rationally. Please accept my apology."

Thank God, she seems to buy it. Or, at the very least, she seems willing to let it go.

"Thank you," she says. "Let's continue, shall we? And if you feel your temper starting to get the better of you again, just say 'Red light,' and we can stop and give you a few minutes to collect yourself. How does that sound?"

How does that sound? It sounds like some infantilizing bullshit for kindergartners.

"Sounds good," I say, pasting on my best smile, the one that women always swoon over.

"So," I continue, in an attempt to redeem myself. "Um, you asked about what happened leading up to me finding Sadie and Mason?"

"I did."

"So, like I said, it was a pretty chill night, nothing out of the ordinary. I mean, Trevor's parties can get pretty wild, and this one was definitely on its way there, but it was still a little early. But then, around ten o'clock, I saw Jayne walk in. And I remember that, because I'd gone to get Sadie a drink maybe ten minutes before, and then when I came back to where we'd been standing, she was gone. I caught sight of her and Liz outside, heading toward the bonfire, and I was just about to follow them when Jayne came in. It was kind of wild for a second, actually, because she and Sadie were dressed exactly alike. I had to do a double take, and while I was doing that, I saw Mason Vreeland walk up to her at one of the jungle juice trash cans."

"Sorry, the what?"

Detective Budd has been taking notes.

"Oh, the, uh, the jungle juice trash cans. It's this mix of Everclear and Kool-Aid and some other stuff, and then Trevor just puts it in these big cans—"

She looks genuinely horrified. "Got it. No more details needed there, thanks."

"So, anyway, Mason and Jayne talked for a minute or so, and it was clear she was super uncomfortable with whatever he was saying to her. She seemed to dodge her way out of the conversation as fast as possible. It was a major red flag to me that she was there, because Sadie had mentioned that Jayne had been calling and texting her earlier in the night with some story that their parents were coming home early and Sadie had to leave. We thought Jayne was just trying to ruin the fun, but when she actually walked through the door, I knew she was serious. So I figured I should find Sadie and Liz ASAP."

"Interesting. Miss Cooper did mention being cornered by Mason Vreeland last night."

I nodded. Our stories were lining up. That helped me relax a little.

"I'm not surprised. Like I said, I don't know what they were talking about, but she was clearly put off by the whole exchange. If she hadn't been able to get away from him, I would have stepped in, but she seemed to be able to handle herself. Jayne is like that."

"Yes, I've gathered as much. So, you went outside . . . ?"

"Oh yeah." I can feel myself gaining momentum as I'm telling the story. I have Detective Budd's undivided attention, and I find myself thinking again that she's still pretty hot, even though she must be close to my dad's age. Maybe a few years younger. But it feels good to have her staring at me like this, closer to how I'm used to being treated by women her age.

I bet this is how she looked at my dad back when she was interrogating him.

"So, I went outside to find Liz and Sadie and let them know Jayne was there. It was a little bit of a relief, honestly, because I was already thinking I'd have to call an Uber to get the two of them back to Sadie's place. Jayne was doing her thing in the house, and as far as I could tell, Mason had wandered off to go creep out someone else. When I got to the bonfire, I found Liz pretty easily, but she said that Sadie had gone back inside to get us more drinks. That's when I got this knot in the pit of my stomach, like I just knew something was really wrong. I'm not going to lie to you, Detective, I'd had a few drinks by then, and I'd downed another beer on my walk to the bonfire."

"You had time to down a whole beer just going from inside to outside?"

I shake my head. She doesn't know how Trevor's works.

"You probably haven't been out to the McClain property, Detective, but it's huge. A walk from the house down to the old field where Trevor usually has a bonfire going is nearly five minutes. It takes a long time, and it takes a long time going back to the house too. But that's what I was doing—heading to the house, because that's where Liz said Sadie had gone. Sadie was drinking a lot that night, probably because Liz was pouring and not just me, and I was a little worried about her wandering up to the house on her own. I just assumed I'd catch up with her somewhere along the way, and I could help her back, and get her into a car and safely home before the Coopers got back."

"Okay, so you were on your way back up to the house—"

God, can this woman let me finish a sentence?

"Yeah," I cut in quickly. "Yeah. I was on my way back up to the house, and there's this old stone barn that the McClains don't use anymore kind of off to the right if you're heading back toward the house. It's kind of the place you go to at his parties if you want to hook up. No one bugs anybody they see walking over there. And for some reason, I thought I caught sight of Mason heading in that direction."

I pause for dramatic effect.

"I'll never forgive myself for not following him in that very minute. But how could I have known that he wasn't alone? That he'd already somehow tricked Sadie into going in there to meet him? I can't guess what was going on in that psycho's head, Detective. I have no idea if he thought Sadie was Jayne, and somehow thought she was the one he got into the barn. I'll never know how he got her there in the first place. You can't know a thing like that; it's impossible. It's—"

"Mr. Carrera, I know how upsetting it must be to relive

this, but please try to stay on track. Just speak clearly and plainly. You were heading back to the house to find Sadie, and you saw Mason Vreeland heading for the barn. But you kept going back up to the house?"

I nod, feeling my leg starting to shake under the table. "Right. Yeah. I just kept thinking I'd find Sadie somewhere along the way. But when I got back to the house, the only person I saw was Jayne. I asked her if she'd seen Sadie, and she said that Sadie had come back inside briefly, but before Jayne could get to her, she'd walked out the door again. Jayne didn't look good. I asked her if she was feeling okay and that's when she said that she had this horrible feeling in her stomach. It hit her after she saw Sadie leave. She told me we had to get out to the barn right away."

"So the two of you went to the barn together?"

"Yes. We ran at full speed, Detective. I swear to God. Jayne started running, and I followed her. I kept asking her why we were sprinting, but I don't think she answered me. I think we both just had a feeling . . . like we had to get to the barn to see if Sadie was there with Mason."

I pause for another moment and meet Detective Budd's eyes, willing myself not to blink.

"Have you ever had your worst fear come true?" I ask. My goal is to disarm her, and it works, if just for a split second.

"I can't say that I have," she replies.

"Well, then." I shrug. "I can't really expect you to understand what I did once I got inside that barn. Because something way worse than my worst fear was there, right in front of me."

"Can you describe to me exactly what you saw?"

I take a deep breath. My leg needs to stop shaking. I focus again on the green tape on the floor. I am here. Now. I may be recounting what happened last night, but I do not live in last night. That's the past. I live in the now. That's what leaders do. They live in the present; they don't get stuck in the past or bogged down by the future. They make decisions for the now. It's the job of the followers to clean up after them.

"I thought I was going to walk in on them hooking up. I don't know why I thought that, but that's what I was afraid of. Sadie was the kind of girl every guy in school wanted, you know? So I was always looking over my shoulder in a way, wondering if some other guy was trying to steal her away. Sometimes I got a little jealous—not that Sadie ever gave me a real reason to be . . . just the usual high school bullshit, you know? So, anyway, I thought I'd walk in on a hookup. What I saw was so much worse. I saw Mason standing over Sadie. He was standing over her, and he had this knife in his hand—I don't know where he got it, but I could see it even though there was almost no light in the barn, and I could see . . ." *Get it together, Carrera. This is the important part.* "I could see that there was blood on it."

My voice catches in my throat.

"I'd call red light," I say finally, "but I need to keep going."

Detective Budd nods. "Just get it out however you need to, Mr. Carrera."

I put my head in my hands. I can't even look at her for the next part.

"I could see that there was blood on it," I repeat. "And for a second, I just couldn't understand it. I couldn't make sense of what I was seeing, because how was it possible? But then I realized it was Sadie on the floor of the barn. That old, dusty, shitty floor. It's where barn animals used to stay, and she was just lying there . . . and she was bloody too. So I put it together, and I just—I attacked him."

Detective Budd nods. She isn't taking notes now. I know because even though I haven't looked up, I can't hear her pen scratching.

"There was a struggle?"

"Yes. Jayne got there a few seconds before I did, but she seemed kind of frozen or in shock or something. I didn't know what else Mason was going to do, so I just lunged at him. He got in a few good swipes at me before I was able to get the knife away from him and Jayne grabbed it from the floor. He didn't stop, though. I thought he was going to kill me. So we fought, and I got him pinned to the ground, but he was still struggling, and so I . . . I strangled him, Detective. Because it was either him or me, and I sure as shit wasn't going to let it be me."

"And where was Jayne during all this?"

To be honest, her response catches me off guard. I was expecting a little bit more sympathy. Maybe even a hand extended across the table. But Sloane Budd appears to be all business.

I finally look up again. "To be honest, I blacked out a little bit, but when I got myself back together, Mason Vreeland was dead, and Jayne was holding Sadie. I don't know if she was already gone by then, but I ran over to them, and I held Sadie too, and I just . . . I told her that I loved her. That it would be okay, that she was safe."

There are tears welling up behind my eyes now, and I let them fall. Best for Detective Budd to see it, to see this side of me too. It will help erase that I called her a bitch a few minutes ago.

"I lied to her, Detective," I say. "Because of course it wasn't going to be okay. She might not have even heard what I was saying, but I couldn't let her die without telling her I loved her. Without telling her that she wasn't alone, and putting my arms around her, and just . . . being with her in that last moment."

I'm not sure what I'm expecting Detective Budd to say. Something sympathetic, maybe? Something thoughtful and kind that ends with some version of the phrase "you're free to go"? Women are supposed to have a sixth sense about these kinds of things, aren't they—emotions or whatever?

"Thank you, Mr. Carrera," she says simply. And nothing else.

"Um . . ." I let a few minutes pass before I speak again, waiting for her to add to that statement. She doesn't. "What happens next?" I ask finally.

"Next? Well, that depends on the continued conversations I need to have with Miss Stratton and Miss Cooper."

"I don't understand. What does that have to do with me?"

She heaves a sigh, as if speaking to me is a burden. I ball my hands into fists. God, I hate it when people are disrespectful like that.

"It has to do with you because I need to know that your stories line up. You and Miss Cooper are the only witnesses we have to exactly what happened between Sadie and Mason, and by your own admission, it seems like Miss Cooper is the one *sober* witness we have. I understand Miss Stratton didn't arrive at the barn until a few minutes after all this had happened."

"Yeah. Yeah, that's right. She was the first one who came running when Jayne started screaming. But I wouldn't trust her account of the night if I were you."

"Oh, no? And why is that?"

I shrug. "Because she's a liar."

The detective arches an eyebrow at me. "That's a bold

statement, Mr. Carrera. Perhaps bolder than you realize. Do you mean that she is a liar, or that she is a person who tells lies?"

What the hell kind of question is that? What am I, a psychiatrist?

"I mean what I said. She's a liar. I'm not trying to be a dick about it. Obviously, you know what happened between me and Liz. But she wouldn't leave me alone after that, even though she promised Sadie she would. And she makes a big deal about how she stopped drinking after the party last year, but she was drunk last night."

"Are you certain of that?"

"I was with her and Sadie for most of the night, and we were *all* drinking. Liz was no exception. Honestly, I was kind of grateful when Jayne showed up to get Sadie, because Liz was supposed to be her ride home, and she clearly wasn't going to be in a state to drive. Guess that should have been the least of my worries, huh?"

"You couldn't possibly have known what was going to happen, Mr. Carrera. But thank you for sharing these details with me. It's very helpful."

Finally, a statement that sounds like it could actually mean the end of this interrogation. Because I don't care what the police call it—"questioning" or whatever. It was an interrogation. I know enough about how girls are all obsessed with true crime to know that they always think the boyfriend did it.

Well, I've said what I have to say to this woman. And she can't prove that everything last night didn't happen exactly the way I say it did.

"You're free to go, Mr. Carrera," she says after a beat. "For now. Thank you for your time. I'm sure your father is anxious to get you home."

I find myself staring at the green tape on the floor just one more time. Marking the moment. Staying in the present. No need to look forward, and sure as hell no need to look back.

"Thanks," I say finally.

I can feel Detective Sloane Budd's eyes following me as I walk out the door.

LIZ

I'M STILL WAITING for Jayne to actually say something to me and not just stare at me like she loathes the very fact of my existence.

"Um, hello?" I say. "Earth to Jayne?"

"I'm here to find Sadie, obviously," she says. "Do you know where she is?"

The fact that Jayne came to Trevor's to find Sadie is completely baffling to me. But something tells me that if I ask a clarifying question, Jayne is going to rip my head off.

"I don't know, actually. I was just with her and Ben, but I think they went out to the bonfire."

Without another word, Jayne pushes past me, presumably in the direction of the bonfire. I don't think she's ever been to Trevor's before, but it isn't exactly hard to spot the massive blaze of fire about a quarter mile out in the field.

I'm about to follow Jayne when I feel a hand on my shoulder. Turning around, I realize the hand belongs to Ben.

"Hey," he says. "Can we talk?"

This is, quite literally, the last thing on earth I need. Somehow I've managed to avoid having a direction conversation with Ben for the past six months, which has been no small feat. Sure, I'm always around when he and Sadie are hanging out, but it's kind of a group thing, you know? It's surprisingly easy to say hello to someone and then commit to not speaking another word to them without anyone else noticing. I perfected the technique with Levi. It definitely only works on guys, though, because they're too stupid to realize that's what you're doing. A girl would pick up on it in less than a minute—Sadie noticed, and I think she appreciated it.

"I really don't think we have anything to talk about," I say, scanning the room and hoping desperately that Sadie is about to walk back through the door.

"You and I both know that isn't true. Our text messages say otherwise."

"I don't want to talk about that."

"Come on, Liz." Ben widens his eyes and gives me a look like he's a puppy. "It's killing me, how things are between us right now. Please have a drink, and let's just talk."

I bite my lip. This is probably a bad idea. Scratch that—this is definitely a bad idea. But maybe, just maybe, it'll put an end to the texting, and the weirdness, and all the things that I like to ignore when I pretend to Sadie that everything is back to normal. It would be nice if I wasn't lying to her when I said that.

"Okay," I say. "Yeah. Let's talk."

"And you were not drinking last night, is that correct, Miss Stratton? I just want to make absolutely certain of that, because your eyewitness account of what you saw when you came into the barn is very important."

"Right."

I take the drink Ben is holding out to me, and he smiles. It's the kind of smile that shouldn't make my stomach flutter, but I wasn't kidding when I told him over spring break last year that he was the hottest guy in Sadie's life. Hell, he's the hottest guy in all our lives. And I hate myself, because I should be better than this. Stronger than this.

And yet . . . Sadie has it all. I can have some of that too, can't I? Don't I deserve it?

The truth is, I don't even remember what happened between me and Ben at the party last year. I was so drunk, and so was he, and it just sort of happened. Like one little feather landed on the scales and tipped everything in a different direction.

In one gulp, I down whatever is in the cup. It tastes like a mix of some kind of hard liquor and lemonade—definitely more of the liquor.

"So," I say, feeling a warming sensation down my throat and into my stomach. As Sadie would say, my sour side is about to come out. Haven't I punished myself enough for what happened last year? If Ben wants to talk, that's his decision. Let Sadie ask him about it later. I've spent the past five years making every single one of Sadie's problems one of my problems. I felt like that's what I owed her for becoming my friend, for letting me be part of her family.

But suddenly, all at once, I feel absolutely done with thinking that way. Friends shouldn't owe each other anything for being in each other's lives.

"What did you want to talk about?"

The thing is, there are some truths that just wouldn't help anybody to know. I have enough life experience to understand that, and I have to imagine that Detective Budd does too. She'd understand why I need to tell her I was sober last night. What does it have to do with anything that I took a drink from Ben? I can't imagine he's eager to share that part of the story or the conversation we had afterward. What does it matter that I grabbed another one on our way out to the bonfire, and got sidetracked talking to someone else, and lost track of Ben?

What does matter is what I saw later that night. And I know what I saw, drinks or not. That is the only thing that's important.

"Okay, so you were at the bonfire around ten thirty, is that right?"

"I'd say so, yeah."

"And did you see Sadie anywhere, or Mason?"

"No, I'd lost track of Sadie. I saw Mason a few times that night, but he seemed totally normal. It all seemed totally normal. The whole night. There was nothing that made me think—" I try to steady my breath.

"It's all right, Miss Stratton. Take your time."

"There was nothing that made me think that what was about to happen was going to happen. I mean, Sadie made fun of Mason a little in junior high, you know? But everyone did. He was a really weird, dorky kid. It was just teasing and stuff, though. Nothing to have made him turn into a homicidal maniac. She didn't mean anything by it, but maybe he took it personally or something. Maybe they had a conversation last night that I didn't see . . ."

I pause to collect my thoughts. It's hitting me all over, like a ton of bricks, just how much this doesn't make any sense at all.

"I just can't make sense of it, really, because if you had asked me before last night, I would have told you Mason was fine. Nice. A little strange and artsy, but also really cute in an under-the-radar kind of way. I think I even remember Sadie mentioning at the start of the school year how cute he'd gotten over the summer. Yeah, she did say that, because it was after she mentioned it that I noticed he'd definitely gotten hot over the summer. Not my type—he was too 'pretty' for me. But . . .

"I thought he was nice, Detective. Nice and cute. What is wrong with me? I should have seen it. I should have known. But I just didn't."

I can't help it anymore. I break down in tears. Again.

"It's all my fault, because I should have known. And I was feeling kind of annoyed with Sadie anyway, and I spent my time talking to Ben instead of tracking her down because it felt kind of good to have the attention, you know? But in that amount of time, and after I went back to the bonfire and couldn't find her—"

I'm sobbing now. I can't actually remember the last time I cried before last night, but this has to be some kind of record.

"I'm her best friend, and she needed me, and I just ghosted her. I left her alone, and look what happened."

Detective Budd is silent while I collect myself, although she does me the courtesy of handing over a mini packet of tissues, the kind you get at a drugstore on your way to a funeral because you suddenly realize you're going to need them. I don't bother saying thank you, but I use every single tissue in the packet.

I'm expecting some kind of punishment now, or maybe she's going to scoff at me like Detective Norris did and tell me I'm an idiot for thinking all this is my fault. There's nothing adults love more than trivializing teenage feelings. It's like a blood sport for them.

"Miss Stratton," she says finally, "I want you to hear me loud and clear here. If what you're telling me is true, then absolutely none of this is your fault. It's impossible to anticipate the actions of someone else, especially an individual as clearly disturbed as Mason Vreeland. Who knows? If you had been with Sadie at the time, he might have simply decided to attack both of you. There's no way to know."

She pauses for a moment, staring me down. "If, however, any part of what you've told me turns out to be untrue, you will be held accountable. Do you understand?"

Shit. She can't possibly know about the drinking, can she? No, no way. I'm just being paranoid. And anyway, that had nothing to do with what I remember.

"Is there something, specifically, you're talking about?" I ask. "Because I'm pretty much an open book. Just ask."

"You've already answered every question I had for you, Miss Stratton. Do you think you've answered those questions to the best of your ability?"

I feel myself starting to turn red under her stare. There's no reason to be flustered, but somehow I feel like I've suddenly been hooked up to a lie detector test, and I can't even remember if I'm telling the truth about my own name.

"Yes, ma'am," I reply quietly. Generally, I'm not one for formalities like "sir" and "ma'am," especially because they play into a certain Southern girl expectation. But Detective Budd has earned it. My instinct was right about her when she first walked into the room. I respect this woman, even if she seems to be trying to read between the lines I didn't even write.

"Okay, then. Now, the last thing I need from you is understanding what happened after you got to the barn last night. What made you go out there in the first place?"

I take a deep breath. This is the hardest part, obviously. Going through yesterday afternoon, reliving what happened when Sadie and I first got to the party . . . all that is harmless, almost fun. I can pretend I'm not here right now, that I'm draped over Sadie's bed the morning after the party, and we're both nursing hangovers and gossiping about what happened the night before.

Going into this part of the night crushes that little daydream with a sledgehammer.

"Do you have any more of those little tissue packets?" I ask suddenly. "I might, uh, need more."

"Sure," she says, producing another one from the pocket of her oversized blazer.

"Thanks."

"You're welcome. Please continue."

It sounds gentle when she says it, but I know an order when I hear one.

"So I was talking with Ben for a while, like I said, and then he stayed up at the house and said he was going to track down Sadie while I went back down to the bonfire. I told him I thought she was outside somewhere, but he kept insisting she was in the house."

"So you and Ben Carrera separated at that time? He didn't walk back down to the bonfire with you?"

"No."

"Did you see him down there later?"

"Um, no. No, I'm pretty sure he was in the house the whole time. Probably trying to find Sadie, like I was. But I didn't see her anywhere."

"Did you see Mason Vreeland?"

I rack my mind, but I can't remember. I shrug. "I had no reason to be paying any attention to him."

The detective nods, scribbling away in her notebook. "Go on."

"I guess close to eleven or so, I figured I should try harder to find Sadie and Jayne. At that point, I thought Jayne had probably tracked Sadie down herself, and they'd left without me."

"Did you try calling and texting Sadie?"

"No." I pause for a moment as I try to remember why I didn't just text her. Then I remember. "I don't think she had her phone with her. I'm not sure what happened to it, but I remember her saying a while after we got to the party that she couldn't find it."

"She had her phone on her when she was found," Detective Budd informs me.

I shrug. "She must have found it. But like I said, last I knew, she'd put it down somewhere, or Ben borrowed it or something, and she didn't know where it was. Is that important?"

"No, it's okay. Please continue."

"Um, I was just starting back up to the house when I heard screams coming from the old barn. There was music and stuff playing by the bonfire, but once you got a little bit away from it, everything faded a lot. You have to pass by the old barn to get back to the house. It's where everyone goes to hook up, you know? So generally, you steer clear of it unless you have something or someone in particular in mind. Anyway, I was still kind of far away from it, but then I heard this horrible screaming. Like, I never got what the word 'bloodcurdling' meant, but then I heard this. It was so awful, and I just started running for the barn."

"You ran toward the scream?"

"Well, yeah. Like I said, that barn is where people go to hook up, and my first thought was that some asshole had a girl in there and was doing something awful to her. I didn't really have a plan; I just thought that bursting in would probably startle the guy enough to stop what he was doing."

"I admire the spirit of the action."

"Yeah." I shake my head. I notice that I haven't actually used any of the tissues in the new packet Detective Budd gave me, but I am slowly shredding the label off it. "What I saw when I got in there, though . . . I'll never forget it for the rest of my life. God, it was so awful."

"Can you describe it for me, please?"

"I ran inside, and it was pretty dark in there, just one old light at the top of the hayloft. But I saw Sadie on the ground, covered in blood. Ben was holding her and sort of rocking back and forth, but he wasn't making any noise. Mason was lying nearby, and I don't know if he was bloody, but I knew without even looking at him real close that he was dead. And there was Jayne. She was the one screaming. Her whole body was shaking, and she had her phone out—I think she was trying to call nine one one, or maybe she already had. But service is so shitty out there. And I remember being confused at first. I thought it must be Jayne who was dead, and Sadie who was alive, screaming her head off. It just had to be."

"Is there a particular reason you thought that?"

"No. No, no, no," I say, uncertain of why I'm repeating myself so many times. "No. I just—my brain didn't compute. I just couldn't believe it was Sadie. I guess maybe because they were dressed alike last night, you know? I just thought that Ben had to be confused. He thought he was holding Sadie, but it couldn't be. Sadie had to be alive. He had to be holding Jayne. He just had to be. He had to be."

I whisper the words the last time I say them. Suddenly every ounce of adrenaline that's probably been coursing through my veins since last night is gone. I have nothing left.

"I need to lie down," I say, and my voice sounds muffled to my own ears.

"I'm sorry. We don't have a—"

"It's fine," I say. Without another word, I slide out of my chair and lie down, flat on my back, on the cold, filthy linoleum floor. There's nothing to stare at but the fluorescent lights above, and I try to take a deep breath. Hell, I try to take any kind of breath at all.

This isn't how it was supposed to be. I want to scream. I want to pound my fists against the floor and yell until my voice is gone. None of this is how it was supposed to be.

It was supposed to be me and Sadie, best friends forever. No one else, and nothing else. Just us, forever. Even though she drove me absolutely crazy. Even though she could be a complete bitch, and I hated the way she teased me and manipulated everyone around her.

People grow. They change. I figured she'd grow up in college, and we'd be middle-aged women guzzling chardonnay, talking about how awful we used to be.

But that isn't what the future looks like anymore. It's gone, forever. Just like that stupid necklace she gave me that ended up meaning so much. Probably lost in the cornfield or charred up in the remains of Trevor's bonfire. It was cheap, anyway. Not meant to last. But I thought it would.

"Miss Stratton." Detective Budd is crouching down on the floor next to me, offering a manicured hand. "We're done with your questioning for now. You're free to go. And I do need you to get up off this floor."

I take her hand and feel momentarily dizzy when I finally stand up again.

"Is there someone we can call for you?" she asks. Normally the amount of pity in her voice would tick me off, but I'm too tired and miserable to care.

"No," I say, shaking my head. "No. No one."

A look of concern passes over her face, but I see it easily replaced with professionalism.

"Well," she says. "If you do . . . need someone, I'll make sure you get the card for the juvenile therapist on staff here."

I need a therapist like I need a kick in the head.

"Thanks," I say, more out of habit than meaning.

"I'm very sorry for your loss, Miss Stratton. And I know it may seem tempting to—how do I put this—get out of Dodge. But please don't go far. Go home, and plan to stick around here for the foreseeable future. In case we have more questions. Can you do that?"

She phrases it like I have a choice. We both know I don't. And my immediate future includes a hell of a lot more Levi and Mel than I ever wanted in my life.

"Yeah," I say simply.

"We appreciate your cooperation, Miss Stratton."

"Cooperation" is an interesting choice of words. But, hey, she's the one in charge. She can call it what she wants.

She's staring at me so intensely that I feel like I'm still on trial for something. I know she said I'm free to go, but her stare indicates otherwise.

"Um, is there anything else?" I ask finally.

Detective Budd heaves a sigh, and suddenly she looks very tired. "Just take care of yourself, Miss Stratton. I know that can seem like an impossible task when the people around you who are supposed to do it don't hold up their end of the deal. But you're worth the effort. I hope you remember that."

I look down at the floor. What am I supposed to say to that? I guess it's a nice idea, whether she means it or not.

"Thanks," I mutter.

She gives a brief nod, like she's satisfied that her job here is done. She has successfully imparted her hard-won wisdom to the troubled teen who reminds her of herself or whatever.

"See you around," I say. And I hope to God I don't.

JAYNE

"SO, YOU TALKED to Mason for a while, he gave you the creeps, and then you made your way outside to the bonfire?"

"Right. I really just wanted to find Sadie and get the heck out of there. Based on when our parents texted, we had maybe an hour and a half until they got back, and it was making me nervous."

"Are your parents strict?"

I shrug. Haven't we gone over all this already?

"They're normal," I reply. "My dad tends to be a little more lax than my mom. He was really popular back in his high school days, and he likes to encourage me and Sadie to go out and let loose a little bit. My mom draws a hard line, although Sadie crossed it a lot. I'm not sure if my parents really knew about half the stuff Sadie and Liz got up to, or if they did, maybe they decided to ignore it because they were trying to give Liz the benefit of the doubt. You know, tell themselves that Sadie was going to be a good influence on her or whatever."

"What about you?"

"I would think it's pretty clear by now, Detective, that I have approximately zero interest in the usual high school stuff. As far as I'm concerned, it's just a four-year sentence I have to go through until I can get to college and get out of this town."

"Yes, I did start to pick up on that. So, back to the party . . ."

The bonfire is blazing, and the heat coming from it takes my breath away. I start scanning the crowd for Sadie, looking for Ben first, since I'm more likely to see his tall head sticking up above everyone else. Something about the conversation I just had with Mason really doesn't sit right with me, and I'm starting to worry that Sadie was playing one of her classic games and she messed with the wrong kid.

"When you say 'one of her classic games,' what do you mean?"

Ugh. I would prefer that this not even come up, but it's also increasingly clear that I can't really talk about what happened last night without talking about some of Sadie's . . . darker tendencies.

"She liked to mess with people," I say. "She never meant anything by it. I don't want you to think she was some kind of mean girl, but there were these games she liked to play, especially with boys. Sadie and I were both really awkward in grade school and middle school. We got made fun of a lot for having red hair, and freckles, and being too pale when all the other girls started tanning in junior high. That kind of thing. But then, in eighth grade—I don't know how else to put this—we got cute. Grew into ourselves, I guess you could say. And I enjoyed it, sure, but Sadie relished it. Then, a few years later, she got together with Ben, and it was like she entered the social stratosphere."

"Did you ever feel envious of that?"

I laugh before I can stop myself. "Sorry. It's just that we're twins. I wasn't jealous of her looks or style, because I have looks and style. And as far as her being the literal homecoming queen, I don't mean to sound disrespectful, because I love my sister, but I just could not possibly care less. It's sort of like asking me if I'd like to be the queen of the dump. It's still a dump, even if you're sitting on the highest pile of trash."

This time it's Detective Budd who laughs.

I smile. Okay, so I was right to like this woman a little bit. "You know what I mean, don't you?" I ask.

"Let's just say that I certainly got out of Dodge myself the minute I could."

"And you probably don't care about whether or not you were the most popular girl in high school, do you?"

"Not a lick."

"And you're probably more successful now than everyone else you went to school with, aren't you?"

Detective Budd shrugs. "That may indeed be the case. But I don't keep up with anyone, so I wouldn't know."

"You and I are very much alike."

She nods and makes a few more notes. For a moment, there is no sound in our room except the scratch of her pen.

"Tell me, what kind of game do you think Sadie was playing with Mason?"

"She knew that he'd asked me out a month or two ago and that it really creeped me out. Maybe she wanted to get revenge on him or make him feel stupid; maybe she was pretending to be me to play a trick on him and make him think that I wanted to get together with him after all. And then he could have found out and gotten angry. Or he could have thought it was me all along. She could have started it, and then he took it too far—"

Seconds ago Detective Budd and I were bantering like we were in some kind of movie, but as I start to talk about what I think could have happened to Sadie, all the air goes out of the room.

For a minute, I forgot this was real. For a minute, I was just having fun going toe to toe with someone who has a brain worth its weight. For a minute, it was all fun and games.

"Jayne? Can you continue?"

I take a deep breath. Of course I can continue. I have to. This is the important part.

Evan and I are still texting, and I'm sending him photos of the bonfire and the old barn illuminated in the background. Given that he lives in Palm Springs, Evan quite literally can't wrap his head around the idea that kids in the Midwest actually party in cornfields. I wish I could say it wasn't true, and up until tonight, even I couldn't verify it with photographic evidence, which Evan tends to demand for everything. But now I'm here, and he is clearly reveling in what appears to him like the absolute absurdity of the heartland.

I put my phone away. Evan can be a little bit demanding, and every so often, I get annoyed at his almost gleeful disdain for people and things that he sees as beneath him on the scale of culture. Although, as long as he and I are on the same level, I guess I can't complain too much. After all, it's hard to find people who truly understand you.

But Evan is going to have to wait. I still haven't been able to find Sadie, and I'm starting to panic a little bit. Finally, I spot Liz on the other side of the bonfire. I weave my way through the crowd of people and grab her arm.

"Shit!" she says, spilling some of her drink. It smells strong. "Jayne, you scared me!"

"Are you telling me that the first time you saw Miss Stratton at the party, it was around ten thirty at the bonfire?"

"Yeah, that's right."

"You didn't see her or speak to her before that time?"

"No. I'm sure she was around, but I didn't see her until I got down there, and I asked her if she'd seen Sadie or Ben because we really had to get going. She was a little drunk, and she got weird when I mentioned Ben. Given their history, I didn't think too much of it, although I was surprised that she was drinking, given what a big deal she made about giving it up and all that. I'm not trying to get her in trouble. I just—I don't know what she was up to last night exactly, and Liz can get super emotional when she drinks, so just knowing how she reacted when I asked about Ben and how she didn't know where Sadie was . . . I'm not trying to imply anything; I just wouldn't trust her memory of everything that happened last night."

"I see. So what did you do after you spoke to Miss Stratton?"

"I mean, no offense to Liz, but I realized she would be pretty useless to me as far as finding my sister, so I started to walk back up to the house. I was calling and texting Sadie the whole time, but I still had no response from her. I feel guilty saying this now, but I was starting to get really angry. Here

I was, dragging myself through a field in the middle of the night, just because I was trying to save my sister from getting in trouble with our parents, and she didn't even have the decency to respond to one of my texts."

Putting my head in my hands, I take a few more deep breaths. "It's really awful," I say, my voice muffled, "to know that while my sister was being killed by some psychopath, I was angry at her. That was the emotion I felt. That's what I was directing at her. Anger. If only I'd known."

"It was impossible for you to know, Jayne. No matter how strong your connection was."

"But that's the thing," I say. "When I was on my way to the house, I got this feeling. Honestly, it was like a stabbing pain in my gut. It probably sounds crazy to you, but I knew in that moment that my sister was in serious danger. And when I looked out at the old barn, I saw that there was a light on in it. I tend to pay good attention to my surroundings, and I just knew the light wasn't on when I was walking down to the fire."

"And you decided to investigate?"

"Yeah."

"I understand from Miss Stratton and Mr. Carrera that the barn is where kids go to hook up with one another at Trevor's parties. Why didn't you just assume that's what it was?"

"I told you, Detective, I'd never been to one of Trevor's parties before. I had no idea that's what the barn was for until just now."

I'm annoyed she interrupted the most important part of the story with such an ancillary detail.

"Anyway," I say pointedly, "I was going to head to the barn anyway when Ben showed up out of nowhere and asked if I was okay, because I was practically doubled over on the ground. My stomach hurt so bad. I told him something didn't feel right and I was worried about Sadie, that I thought something bad might be happening in the barn. He agreed to check it out with me, because he didn't know where she was either. We were walking together at first, but the closer we got to the barn, the worse I started to feel, and I just knew something was seriously wrong. So I took off running. I don't know what Ben was thinking—maybe I was panicked and so he got panicked too; we obviously haven't talked about it after everything that happened, so you would have to ask him—but I think on some level, he knew something was wrong too."

I pause and look at Detective Budd, waiting for her to confirm or deny that Ben told her something similar, but she doesn't say anything other than "Go on."

"Okay, so I ran the rest of the way there. The feeling in my stomach—the initial stabbing pain—was gone, but the ghost of it was still there, and I just felt sick with worry. Sadie and I have had that kind of connection before. Like, when my appendix burst in sixth grade, she collapsed, screaming in her chair, in another class at exactly the same time. Turns out her appendix was fine, no issues. But she could literally feel my pain. It's the kind of story my parents still like to tell at parties when people ask what it's like having twins."

"I believe you, Jayne. I deal with the facts, but I'm smart enough to know there's more to the world than what we can see."

"Thanks, Detective. I told the other cops about it earlier too, but I'm pretty sure they just thought I was crazy."

"I would tell you I'm surprised, but frankly, that tracks. But I promise, it would take more than sharing something about your intuition for you to be labeled as crazy in my book."

I nod. We understand each other, me and Detective Budd, and I find myself curious about how she found herself sitting in the chair across from me. Another story, maybe, for another time.

"Can you tell me what you saw once you got to the barn? Take all the time you need."

What I saw once I got to the barn. As she asks the question, I realize for the first time that these memories will be with me forever. What I saw, what happened to Sadie. They will always be with me. I hold on to the necklace she gave me for an extra boost of strength.

"I got there first. Before Ben. And I saw Mason Vreeland," I say. "And at first I thought he was alone and that he was sick or something, because he was hunched over and moving in this weird way. It was scary, and I almost turned around and just left. But then I saw that he was standing over something, and I realized . . . I realized it was her. My sister. She was covered in blood, and he was holding this knife. I just couldn't make sense of it. Sadie was gasping, and then I must have made some kind of sound, because Mason turned to me, and his eyes just looked black. There was nothing there. That's when Ben burst in."

"And then what happened?"

I'm aware that I'm crying, but I don't wipe my tears.

"I was frozen in place," I say. "I can't explain it, but I just stood there. But Ben was so brave. He realized what was happening, and he vaulted toward Mason and pulled him off Sadie. They struggled. Mason was trying to slash him with the knife. I finally came to my senses and ran to Sadie, but there was so much blood. It was too much. I knew it was too much for her to be okay. The next time I looked over at Ben and Mason, Mason was lying still. I think Ben—" I take a deep breath, realizing this is also the first time I'm saying all this out loud. "I think Ben choked him to death. He did what he had to do, Detective. I have no idea what would have happened if he wasn't there. I could be dead now too. Mason could have gotten away with it and be walking around today like nothing even happened. Ben was in such bad shape himself, but he just kind of crawled over to where I was sitting with Sadie, and he held her in his arms, and he"—my voice chokes up—"he just told her that he loved her. And that it would be okay. And that's probably when she took her last breath. It wasn't until I realized that she was really gone that I started screaming. And then I couldn't stop.

That's when Liz came running in—she heard me. And eventually, a lot of the other kids did too, because I couldn't stop screaming. And then someone called the cops. And now here I am, talking to you."

"I'm so very, very sorry for your loss, Jayne. And for what you endured . . . It wasn't your fault."

I look up at her, my vision blurry with tears. "Wasn't it, though?" I ask. "I can't stop going over every detail, wondering what I could have done differently. What if I hadn't told my parents about the party? What if Sadie and Liz just went like it was nothing, and what if I didn't show up there? What if all this happened because Mason thought Sadie was me, and he only thought that because he'd heard I came to the party? What if my dad hadn't forgotten his medication, and my parents hadn't needed to come home early?"

"Sweetheart," Detective Budd says, and I'm surprised by the soft kindness in her voice. "If you keep asking yourself all those questions, you'll never hear yourself think again. It is what it is, and it happened. It's a terrible, awful thing, and I would never suggest that you will get over it. But you can't blame yourself for it. The best way to honor your sister's life is to go live yours the very best way you can."

I take a few minutes to collect myself and consider those words.

"Thank you, Detective," I say finally. "That's really good advice."

"I hope you take it. For your sake, and for Sadie's."

"It might take me some time, but I will. I promise."

Detective Budd nods, satisfied. "Well, I know your parents are anxious to get you home, Miss Cooper. And I know how important it is for you to be together as a family right now. You're free to go."

Just like that, it's over.

"If you need anything," I find myself saying, "or have other questions for me, if there's anything at all I can do . . ."

"I promise, we will reach out. Thank you, Jayne. You've been through enough. Get some rest."

The heavy metal door opens, and I blink at the bright daylight coming through the windows of the station hallway. It's a reminder that the world still exists. That the sun still rose today. That there is a new life to live, and I have the power to choose how to live it.

For Sadie.

When I get outside, Ben is sitting on a bench, waiting. My phone gives a sudden ping, startling me. I had to turn it over to the police when I first got here. I glance down, assuming it's my parents.

Evan's name pops up on the screen. And he has questions.

ACT THREE

DEAD GIRL TALKING

I must be gone and live, or stay and die.
—William Shakespeare, *Romeo and Juliet*

Reserving judgements is a matter of
infinite hope.
—F. Scott Fitzgerald, *The Great Gatsby*

SADIE

ONE MONTH BEFORE THE PARTY

I'VE ALWAYS BEEN obsessed with the 1996 movie *Romeo + Juliet*. You know, the one with Leonardo DiCaprio and Claire Danes. I saw it for the first time in eighth grade, when I had a teacher who clearly never forgave himself for giving up on his dream of being an actor in favor of teaching a bunch of Midwestern kids why they should appreciate Shakespeare. Spoiler alert: He failed at getting about 99.9 percent of the kids to care. I was the .1 percent exception.

God, that movie is gorgeous. It might not even be fair

to say I like Shakespeare. Maybe I just like Baz Luhrmann's version of the play. But either way, after I saw that movie, I became hell-bent on this idea of finding that kind of love. The kind that you'd be willing to die for after just three days together. I know, I know. That story is fiction, and even if it wasn't, it is not exactly a shining example of healthy relationships. But I'm a romantic. Sue me.

For a while, it seemed like I was actually heading for the opposite of a Shakespearean tragedy—my very own fairy-tale ending. After all, by sophomore year of high school, I was dating Ben. *Ben Carrera.* I might not have been willing to drink poison or run a sword through myself for him, but we really had something together. And everyone was so jealous—even Jayne was impressed, and she was usually smart enough to avoid falling into the trap of caring about high school social climbing.

"It's just . . . We're *twins,*" she said to me once, while we were getting ready for a dance together and Ben was waiting downstairs. "What do you have that I don't?!"

"Well, for starters," I said, "I've got Ben Carrera. And better hair."

"You liar!" she said with a laugh. "You do not!"

Jayne can believe what she wants. We might be identical, but my hair is definitely better.

The tricky thing is that somewhere along the line, even

with Ben's arm slung around my shoulder and all our friends laughing at whatever our latest story was—because we always had stories—something just felt *off.*

And that's how it started with Mason Vreeland. I thought Ben was my Romeo, but it turned out he was just my Paris. And just like Juliet, meeting Romeo has turned my entire life upside down.

It should never have even turned into anything, me and Mason. I'd known him since we were kids, and he was always the quiet kind of guy. I didn't have anything against him; I just didn't know him, and I got the sense that no one really did. I think I might have teased him a little in junior high. I don't remember, but he claims I did. God, I was such a brat. Luckily, he says it was never anything really bad.

By the time senior year of high school rolled around, he had definitely transformed from an ugly duckling into a swan, but that didn't change his social behavior. It was strange to have a guy walking around who looked like he could be a movie star but somehow repelled attention and all the trappings of the popularity that should have been his.

But then we both decided to take third-period photography during first semester this year. I've already applied early decision to Loyola in Chicago, and considering that both of my parents are alums, I'm feeling pretty good about it. It's been three years of hard work, and all I want is to take a breath and enjoy a class where getting an A is as easy as showing up and arguing that whatever you decide to take a picture of is actually art.

It was supposed to be a throwaway class. My parents don't even know I'm taking the class—they object to anything that doesn't have what my dad would call "real-world application." I have a hunch he was just saying that to me because photography has always been Jayne's thing. She's in the club and everything, and she's had an interest in it since we were kids and she became obsessed with old movies and Hollywood glamour shots. My dad has always been more likely to speak up for my sister than for me, a fact that I've gotten so good at ignoring that it could practically escape my notice for real. It's been that way for a long time—my dad and Jayne, my mom and me. I couldn't tell you why, but I feel like that probably happens in most families with two kids. Each parent is just naturally closer to the kid who seems more like them.

I've always kind of thought that having kids is super egotistical, and my own family dynamics are doing a pretty good job of supporting the theory. But I digress.

The bottom line is that I just didn't mention it. Photography class, I mean. It wasn't supposed to be a big deal.

Maybe that's how Juliet felt the night she met Romeo.

I was late to class on the first day. It sounds stupid, but I didn't realize until the bell rang that I had no idea where the photography room was. Our school is pretty big, and there's an old basement that they converted into classrooms where I have literally never been before. Turns out, that's also where the photography lab happens to be. After about seven wrong turns, I finally burst into the classroom.

"Sorry," I muttered, scanning the room for an empty seat at the two-person tables. Did this place used to be a chemistry lab? Why was there a sink at the front of the room where the teacher was standing?

The only seat left was next to a guy who looked vaguely familiar to me, and I sat down as fast as I could, clattering my bag to the floor. I might've only been taking this for the A, but I'm still not the kind of girl who likes to be late. Another difference between me and Jayne—she can't be bothered to show up to anything on time to save her life. She just happens to be brilliant enough that no one ever cares. The straight A's that take me hours of studying to achieve seem to just come naturally to her.

"Sorry," I repeated, this time more quietly, to my new seatmate.

He looked at me and smiled. "For what?" he asked, clearly amused. "You're good, Red."

I opened my mouth again to chastise him for the nickname, an annoying nod to my hair that was as eye-roll-inducing as it was unoriginal, but then our eyes met, and he smiled again. Like, actually smiled.

You know how it feels when someone smiles at you, and you know that they're not just doing it to be polite? It's not the kind of smile that they just toss out to a barista, or a cashier, or even their friends. It's a smile for *you.*

I felt myself blush. He was cute, but I got the sense that he either didn't know it or didn't care. Not like Ben. Ben cared *desperately.*

"Thanks," I mumbled.

"Sadie, right?" he asked, holding out a hand. Honestly, who shakes hands in high school?

"Yeah," I replied. "Um—"

"Mason," he said, saving me the embarrassment of having to admit that he obviously knew me, but I didn't know him.

"Right, of course. Hi."

"Hi."

He smiled again.

And I knew at that moment that I was in deep trouble.

Mason and I didn't talk for the rest of class—it was class, after all, and the teacher was preaching to us about the value of physical film in the digital age. But to be honest, if you wanted the specifics of that lecture, I couldn't give them to you. Every single inch of my body was extremely aware that I was sitting next to Mason. God, I couldn't even remember his last name. It started with a *V* . . . Was it "Vaughan," maybe? All I knew was that my heart felt like it was going to beat out of my chest, and it took every ounce of focus I had to keep my cool and look like a normal human being.

I think Mason could tell. And he was enjoying it.

Nothing like this had ever happened to me before, just the immediate chemistry with someone. Ben was hot, obviously, and we had a really good thing going, but there was nothing . . . I don't know, *elemental* about it. Sitting next to Mason was different.

Girl. Get yourself together. My inner voice was firm, and it was right. This was ridiculous. And anyway, it wasn't even really worth thinking about. I sat down next to Mason because it was the only seat left and because I was late. Next class I just wouldn't be late. Easy.

I could forget all about the way he was making my pulse race and the way he smelled like pine and something musky that was definitely a welcome break from the cheap body spray that seemed to hang permanently in the air of the hallways.

When the bell rang, I sprang out of my seat like someone had shocked me. I grabbed my bag and wasn't even planning to say goodbye to Mason (after all, we were seatmates for one period—that was hardly the formal start of even the most casual friendship, was it?). But he put a hand lightly on my arm as I was leaving.

"Hey," he said, and I tried to act like his skin touching my skin hadn't just lit my entire body on fire.

"Yeah?" I replied, failing to sound annoyed and instead just sounding out of breath. God, could I have any less chill?

"If you need help finding the place before next class, I'll be at the top of the stairs by the cafeteria."

That's what he said out loud. The only thing I heard was *I feel this too.*

"Uh, thanks. Pretty sure I can manage now that I've been down here."

Did I sound detached enough? Annoyed enough? Did my voice say, *This is not happening; I have a boyfriend*?

"Right," he replied, and he moved his hand from my arm. "Of course."

Okay, yes. So my voice actually conveyed what I'd meant to say. Or, at least, what I needed him to understand.

I wish I could say that's where the story ended. That I ignored Mason after that, and he ignored me, and I sailed along safely inside the perfect world I'd built for myself, with me and Ben Carrera at the center. That would have been the smart thing to do. After all, who throws their entire carefully constructed life away just because they got goose bumps sitting next to a cute guy in photography class? When has that story ever worked out in the real world?

And yet. Just like Juliet, I couldn't let it go. And just like Romeo, he couldn't either.

Maybe if we'd done things differently, we would both still be alive.

Why is it everything is always clearer in the rearview mirror?

* * *

Mason Vreeland and I developed a routine after that. Neither of us said anything about it, but for the next two weeks, he was waiting at the top of the stairs by the cafeteria before class, and we walked to the photography lab together. We didn't say much (it wasn't a very long walk). Just "Hey" or "How's it going"—the kind of things you say when you don't really expect a response and when you don't want to give a response yourself.

The Monday after homecoming, that changed. When Mason saw me coming down the hall, he gave an exaggerated bow.

"Well, if it isn't the queen herself."

Yes, Ben and I had been crowned homecoming king and queen after the football game on Friday night. No, it wasn't the type of thing I thought Mason would care about.

"Oh, come on, I don't need your crap," I replied. "What's wrong with being homecoming queen, anyway?"

"Nothing," he said as we fell into lockstep on our usual path to class. "It's just a little . . . basic, you know?"

"Do people still say 'basic'?"

"Well, I just said it, and I'm people."

"Fair enough. But I'm still not interested in your opinion on my extracurriculars."

We were walking along one of the deserted basement

hallways, and I was between Mason and a long row of lockers. Without warning, he stopped short and whirled around to face me. I almost ran directly into him.

"What the hell?" I asked. "What's your problem?"

There was no one else around, and suddenly, like a rush, I felt everything I'd felt the first time I'd sat down next to him. Everything that I thought we'd made an unspoken pact to ignore because it wasn't going to lead us anywhere good. He was staring at me, and he was too close. I should have told him to back off. I should have told him that I'd be walking by myself from now on, and he was out of line. I should have told him that he was making me uncomfortable. He was, but for an entirely different set of reasons.

He was making me uncomfortable because he was looking at me with his big dark eyes like he was about to kiss me. And I was uncomfortable because I wanted him to. Deeply. Desperately.

"You could be a lot more than just homecoming queen, you know," he said finally, his voice barely above a whisper. "You don't have to be his girl just because it looks good to everybody else. You don't have to pretend."

"I'm not pretending," I replied, willing my voice to sound annoyed. "You don't even know me."

He cocked his head to one side and bit his lip, studying me. God, he was sexy.

"You really think you're something special, don't you?" I

asked, trying to catch my breath. "Is this your thing, being all moody and quiet and then coming on really strong?"

He laughed. He actually *laughed.* "Something like that."

"You might be the most arrogant jerk I've ever met."

"Really? That's saying something, considering who you're dating."

"Screw you."

I meant to walk away after I said that. The bell had already sounded, which meant we were late. And who did Mason Vreeland think he was, anyway? Just because he was somehow above the high school crap, he thought it was his only purpose in life to rain on everyone else's parade and tell them how he thought they should be acting. I was surprised he and my sister weren't the best of friends—they seemed to have that particular line of thinking in common.

"I don't need anyone telling me who I am, or who I should be, or who I could be," I said finally. "And we're officially very late for class, so if you'll excuse me."

I pushed him out of the way and started down the hallway.

"Tell me you're happy, then," he called after me.

I turned back. "What?"

"Tell me you're happy. Look, I'm sorry if I came off like a jerk, but I just . . . I've gotta know. Are you happy? Because if you are, I'll leave you alone. Scout's honor." He even held his fingers up like a Scout.

"You don't really seem like a Boy Scout to me."

He shrugged and gave me a million-dollar smile. "Until I was twelve. Once a Scout, always a Scout. So, what's your answer?"

"I—" I suddenly felt like I was standing in the hallway completely naked. It was actually none of Mason's business if I was happy. He was the last person on earth who should care, but he was also the only one who was asking.

Damn it.

In my few seconds of silence, Mason had crossed the space between us. The hallway was still empty, so there was no one to see us when he slowly brought his hand to my face.

That was the moment I realized I was not in love with my boyfriend. That was also the moment I kissed Mason Vreeland.

Once Mason and I started seeing each other, I realized just how good I was at lying. I should've known I was good at it, anyway—turns out, I'd been lying to myself for pretty much the entirety of my high school career. But now I was lying to other people, and that was a different game. Luckily, it was a game I was good at.

The one thing in my life that got easier was my relationship with Liz. It had been hard to forgive her after what went down with Ben at the party last year. She swore that she didn't even remember it happening, which somehow made it worse, and I'll never forget the look on Jayne's face when she sat me down in our kitchen the day after the party and told me what she'd seen.

"You're messing with me," I remember saying. "Come on, Jaynie. I know you hate all this high school stuff, but you can't just make up lies about people."

"I'm not lying, Dee. I'm really sorry, but I'm not. I saw it with my own eyes. Evan did too."

Evan. I loved that kid as much as I hated him, and he'd been a singular fixture in Jayne's life ever since they'd met on the show-jumping circuit. He was absolutely incredible in every way, but he was also deeply aware of that fact. Unlike some of the guys in our town, Evan had the money, the culture, and the lifestyle to back up his high opinion of himself. There was even some conversation about him joining the Youth Olympics equestrian team. I'd seen him at a few shows when we'd all traveled with Jayne, and he was amazing. Jayne's friendship with him seemed inevitable after they met. Two peas in a pod, although I could have just as easily seen them becoming mortal enemies or being the kind of people who have crazy sex every time they meet on the show circuit but never speak of it. People that similar are either best friends or sworn to eternal loathing, and I was glad they fell into the first category.

My sister was a tricky person to figure out. I knew her like the back of my hand, but because I knew her, I also understood why she had zero interest in the usual social trappings of our school. Jayne had really big plans (she hated when people called them dreams, because "dreams" implied that they might not come true, and everything she intended to do was absolutely going to happen), and she saw her time in our town as a prison sentence of sorts until she was allowed out into the real world. That's what always annoyed me, because even though she was the one dying to get out, she was also the one my dad seemed to lavish all the attention on. Special access to his office, where literally no one else was allowed, and he was always chatting with her about what was going on with the business, even when it was clear she had no interest.

I, on the other hand, was overflowing with interest. Ben and I had it all figured out. We were going to merge the family development firms as soon as we graduated from college and run a nice little Midwest empire. It was comforting to know that the business was there, like a safety net, no matter what. We'd have money. We'd go on fabulous vacations during the slow season. We'd have a set of twins and live in this gorgeous house on the clock-tower green that I'd admired since I was a little girl. It would be perfect. Yet somehow it almost seemed like the more I wanted it—wanted to learn about the business, get my feet wet, all that stuff—the more my dad resisted. The more he cared what Jayne thought.

Look, show me the kid who can figure out their parents, and I'll show you the kid who will save a fortune in therapy.

At any rate, that's one of the reasons I ended up so close with my mom. She actually showed enthusiasm for the things I cared about, and she threw herself into whatever hobby, project, or relationship drama I was going through. Sometimes I wished she'd be a little more of a parent and less of a friend, but she was trying in her own way. She'd had us young, and I think she missed out a little bit on becoming a fully formed adult with her own ideas and sense of self that were separate from my dad.

Funny thing is, that's exactly where I was headed with Ben, and I couldn't even see it. But I'm getting ahead of myself.

Like I said, Jayne was the one who told me what had happened between Liz and Ben, and Evan backed it up. I remember feeling like the air had been knocked out of my lungs. I just couldn't believe that Ben would do something like that. And Liz? I don't know. I always got the sense that she was a little jealous of me, and maybe that's why we'd become friends in the first place. It pained me to think about it, but I could see her getting drunk and making a move on Ben. What I couldn't believe was that he would go along with it or that they would take it that far. All the way. Sure, Ben and I weren't sleeping together, but he never seemed to me like the kind of spiteful boyfriend who would say, *Fine, I'll get it somewhere else*. Apparently, although he'd never said it, that was how he'd felt. Why else would he have done it?

I remember Jayne wrapping her arms around me while I cried, and I felt a rush of appreciation for my sister. My twin.

"I'm so sorry, Dee," she said. "You don't deserve to go through this. I wish there was something I could say to make it better."

"I just can't believe it. I mean, I believe it, but how could they do this to me? In *public*?"

"They were both drunk. I honestly don't know if they'll even remember it this morning."

"Who started it? Do you know? Did you see?"

Jayne took a deep breath and pulled away from me, looking me in the eyes. Looking in a mirror.

"I'd say it was Liz," she said finally. "I'm not sure if that makes it better or worse for you, but she was all over Ben from the minute he came into the room. Obviously, he messed up, but she sure was making it hard for him to say no."

Then I asked the question I was most afraid of: "Do other people know?"

"Yeah," Jayne said. "I hate to say it, but I think everyone who was at the party knows. And if they all know . . ."

"Then by tomorrow the whole school is going to know," I finished the sentence for her.

This was my literal nightmare.

It was Jayne's idea that I take the next week off. I had finally recovered from Covid, but it was a convenient reason to keep staying home. Jayne said that she was starting to feel sick too, and even though I think my parents had their doubts, they let it slide. Jayne and I used to be inseparable when we were little, but middle school and high school had changed that. We just had different hobbies and different types of people we hung out with—I think they figured that, whether we were really sick or not, a little sibling bonding was exactly what we needed.

It took a few days of nonstop carryout and *Dawson's Creek* binges for me to feel ready to talk to Liz and Ben about what had happened. Jayne was actually the one who told me not to.

"Let them come to you," she said. "They probably don't even know you know. Won't it be interesting to see which one of them decides to come clean first?"

On the one hand, I agreed with her. On the other hand, I hated the fact that apparently neither of them had thought to tell me right when it had happened. And they still hadn't said anything. My phone didn't have a single notification from either of them.

"You're better off without them, anyway," Jayne said. "Liz is basically a parasite on this family—I'm sorry to say it, but it's true—and you can do so much better than Ben Carrera. He's a big fish in a small pond. Go get yourself a damn whale."

I had to laugh at that, which seemed to make Jayne happy. Ultimately, though, I didn't listen. And I think that really ticked her off.

Because a few days later, Liz came clean about what happened. And then so did Ben. The funny thing is that both of them thought that I didn't know yet and seemed to be under the impression that even though Jayne knew, she hadn't said a word to me—in fact, she'd told each of them that if they didn't tell me, she would. But she already had . . . It was one of those moments I sometimes had with Jayne that made me question what was going on in her mind. Between that and the kind of so-called games she and Evan liked to play, manipulating people into doing things just to see if they could . . . I don't know. I just never understood her. She was my twin sister, and in so many ways, we could read each other's minds. But I felt like Jayne knew everything there was to know about me, yet there was still some part of her that I wasn't seeing.

Anyway, the bottom line with Liz and Ben was that the more time I spent talking to each one of them, the more I realized that the entire perfectly balanced equilibrium of our social lives depended on my forgiving them. So I did. It's not like I was being noble about it. To be honest, I just decided that I could ditch Liz after graduation if I felt like it, and I figured that Ben's transgression would just end up being one of those things we talked about ten years from now as the moment he realized I would always be the only girl for him. And, look, it's not like he gave me much of a choice when it came to whether or not we were going to stay together. After we'd talked things out a bit and I told him I wasn't sure if I would stay with him, he literally started showing up at our house night after night, playing "In Your Eyes" from my favorite eighties movie on an honest-to-God boom box. Where do you even find one of those?

After the first night, I begged him to stop. I remember being out in the front yard, crying and pleading with him to just leave and give me the time I needed to process everything. He kept insisting he was out there for *me*, but it felt like he was really out there for himself, so he could feel better about whatever internal dialogue he had going on to prove to himself that he was the sincere, contrite boyfriend. And, of course, he totally ignored my boundaries.

In fact, the next night, he just showed up again, even earlier, playing the music even louder. My parents thought it was a romantic gesture ("He just loves you so much, Sadie. Give him another chance!" I remember my mom saying), and Jayne seemed to think it was hilarious. I hated that—the way my parents just totally dismissed the fact that I felt like Ben was violating my trust all over again by not listening to me telling him to go. And the way Jayne just laughed. She told me it was all she could do given the absurdity of the situation, and she told me that I should be laughing too. But I wasn't.

Anyway, after two more nights of Ben showing up, I finally caved. It was clear he wasn't going to stop, and forgiving him honestly felt inevitable, anyway. Of course we were staying together. We were Sadie and Ben. When you're high school sweethearts and you get together so young, you have to expect some ups and downs. I knew enough about my parents' relationship to know that there were some skeletons buried in the back of their closet, but I also knew enough not to ask about them.

Whatever those skeletons were, they'd put them behind them. And if Steven and Carly Cooper could do that and go on to build the gorgeous life they had, then I could deal with this, right?

I know I'm all over the place here, but the whole reason I dug into the Liz/Ben thing was because, like I said, meeting Mason suddenly made it a lot easier for me to truly, genuinely forgive Liz. Because I stopped caring. It wasn't a gradual thing either. I kissed Mason Vreeland in that basement hallway, and it felt like a light switch turned on for the first time in a room I hadn't even known existed. I could forgive Liz, let go of things with Ben, and just be.

High school isn't that simple, though, is it? And, fine, I'll admit it, I liked having my cake and eating it too. Things with Ben were intense and definitely not always good, but they were also deeply familiar. Our fights followed a pattern; our make-ups followed a pattern. It was like putting on an old sweater that might not look good on you anymore, but it's still the most comfortable thing you own. So you keep it, even when you shouldn't. Mason hated that. I couldn't blame him, but I also couldn't let go of the idea of the perfect life I was going to build with Ben.

It would have been a relief to tell Liz about all this. It's the kind of thing best friends are supposed to tell each other, and I knew more of Liz's deep, dark secrets than anyone honestly should. But I sort of prided myself on not *having* any deep, dark secrets. One of the reasons why being friends with Liz was so easy was because our lives were such total and complete opposites. I always knew I was just a little bit prettier, a little bit smarter, and a whole lot wealthier, and I had this perfect boyfriend too. Liz just had a series of guys who could be referred to on a scale of "mistake" to "psycho."

I liked feeling like I was better than her. Sue me.

And cheating on my longtime boyfriend with the hot art kid definitely did not fit into my idea of moral superiority. What would Liz have done, anyway? Given me advice? Thanks, but no thanks.

This was one secret I planned to take to my grave. But then two things happened that changed my point of view.

First, Mason and I slept together.

And second, Jayne asked Mason out.

* * *

The idea that Jayne would ask out anyone, at all, seemed impossible to me. I knew that she preferred college guys, and she had always shown exactly zero interest in anyone we went to school with. If she were anyone else, I would have written off the "I prefer college guys" line as something that girls say to make themselves feel better about the fact that no one is asking them out. But I knew Jayne hung out at college parties sometimes, and I knew that when she spent time with Evan at his place, she had her fair share of fun (just not with him, which made zero sense to me). If anything, her high-and-mighty act just grated on me. We were literally twins—who the hell was she to think she was too good for guys her own age?

I don't think she ever would have even told me she'd asked Mason out, but I happened to come home from track practice early one day, and I found her sitting at the kitchen table, looking like someone had just told her she had to stay in this town forever. In other words, she looked like her entire world had just ended.

"Jayne? Earth to Jaynie?" I remember waving my hand in front of her face and getting absolutely no reaction.

"Hey," I tried again. "Come on, what's wrong? You're freaking me out a little bit."

She kept staring directly ahead, so I sat down next to her and decided that I would just wait her out. I could be stubborn that way. So could she.

"You're not leaving, are you?" she asked finally, still not looking at me.

"Nope."

"Ugh. Fine. You may as well know, I got rejected today."

For a minute, I was confused. Rejected by what? A college? A grand prix show?

"Oh," I said, "I'm sorry. Do you wanna talk about it?"

I couldn't tell if she was genuinely listening to me, or if she just felt like talking and I happened to be in the room. Jayne was like that sometimes.

"No."

That was the end of the conversation with Jayne, but only the beginning of it with Mason. A few days later, while we were walking to class, he was acting strangely.

"What's going on with you?" I asked. "Everyone is acting so weird lately."

"Jayne didn't tell you?"

"Tell me what?"

"She, um, made a move on me. In the darkroom the other day."

I stopped walking. I knew that Jayne and Mason were in photography club together, but as far as I was concerned, that wasn't a particularly important fact. Apparently, I was wrong.

"That really doesn't sound like my sister. Are you sure you

didn't misconstrue it or something? She's pretty ice-cold most of the time."

"There was nothing to misconstrue, Sadie. She asked me if I wanted to go to this photography show down in Columbus next week and suggested we could get a hotel room and stay the night there."

"Okay, now I *know* you're not talking about my sister."

Mason gave a frustrated sigh. "Look, I didn't want to tell you this, especially because of"—he motioned between us—"you know, *us*, but your sister has had a thing for me for a long time."

"You had better not be about to make this a weird twin thing, because I'm not here to be some kind of sideshow for your fantasies."

If I had a dollar for every time I'd heard a joke from some crass asshole about me and Jayne, I would have enough to buy a beer to pour over all their collective heads. If that was what this was to Mason, then I was one thousand percent out.

"God, no. Sadie, come on. Absolutely not. I get why you would think that, but just . . . no. Please believe me when I say that you and your sister might look alike, but you couldn't be more different. You're gorgeous, and vibrant, and alive, and she's"—he paused, trying to find the right words—"she's just . . . not."

I raised an eyebrow. "Eloquent finish there."

At the joke, he relaxed a little bit. "So you believe me?"

Did I believe him? Yes, of course I did. Because I knew what he meant about Jayne. There was something that just seemed to be missing, even though most people never realized it. If you spent enough time with her, you'd start to catch on. That's what I thought, anyway, and I was relieved to know that Mason saw it too, because not everyone did. In fact, to the whole world, Jayne probably just seemed like the cool, aloof, sophisticated girl who was going places and couldn't be bothered with the town she came from. They wouldn't see anything else, would they? Not unless they were really, *really* looking.

If they did, they would have seen something that even I didn't realize until it was too late. For some people, the darkness just goes all the way down.

I'll admit, what happened next wasn't my proudest moment. Like I said, after Mason and I slept together for the first time, I was dying to tell someone. It felt like a victory, in a weird way. I had gotten him. He was mine. And I was giving Ben a taste of his own medicine, even though he would never find out about it. I would always know. I would know that the score between us was settled.

And it had honestly been incredible. People talk about it being awkward or whatever, but that's not what it was like with us. Admittedly, the water bottle of vodka and lemonade I brought when we met up that night probably helped. But he was also just so . . . gentle. Sincere, I guess, in a way that almost made it hard to stand. I wanted to have sex, not make love. Making love was the kind of thing I was planning to do with Ben on graduation night. The special moment I'd already been planning for, even though it was months away.

Making love felt permanent, like I was making some kind of unspoken promise to Mason that I already knew I was going to break. Because by then things had already started to change a little bit. Mason had started out as something exciting, exotic. I thought I'd finally understood what love was. But it turns out, it might have been more like lust. To put it another way, I realized why the entirety of *Romeo and Juliet* took place in less than a week. Any longer and Juliet probably would have come to her senses and married Paris. Even if she decided to keep Romeo on the side.

When we were done, tangled up in his sheets, he took out his camera and snapped a close-up. He promised me it wasn't even of my face, just a few locks of hair around my neck. My necklace too, the BFF necklace I got Liz for Christmas the year before, and then I had to run out and buy an extra one for Jayne when she lost her shit over me giving it to Liz and not her. "We're *twins*," she'd kept insisting.

The funny thing is, I know she didn't actually, really care.

She just cared about Liz having something that she didn't have. Nothing bothered Jayne more. It was such a pain to go back out to the holiday market the day after Christmas and scour the jewelry stall to see if they still had another one. Luckily, they did. And it was half-price. Jayne wasn't even grateful when I came home and gave it to her. She just gave me a look that said *Finally, you've gotten it right,* and took it upstairs to her room. It wasn't even her style, way more "camp" than Jayne likes to go, but she did wear it sometimes, usually when she knew that Liz was going to be around. Just to remind her, I guess, that she had the twin card *and* the necklace.

Anyway, telling Liz about me and Mason was off the table, and I really didn't have any other close friends I could trust with something that big. The only person I could think of was Jayne.

Part of me wanted to confide in her because she was my sister, and because when the chips were down or something major happened to either of us, we had each other's backs. Heck, when I got appendicitis when we were younger, Jayne even faked that she had it too so that she could get pulled out of school and we could be together. It's funny; we told my parents that she got stomach pains at the exact same time I did even though we were in different classes, and they actually believed us. We said it was a "twin thing," which was our favorite way of getting around rules or explaining how we knew things we weren't supposed to know.

My parents still like to tell that story at parties. They have no idea it's a lie. And they also don't know that while Jayne did that partly to hang out with me after surgery, she mostly did it because she didn't want to finish the big project that was due as part of our US history unit on the Civil War. This was just a convenient way to get an extension and for her to rewatch *Gone with the Wind* (she's always been weirdly obsessed with old movies) for the fifth time and say it was for class.

I knew that Jayne would help me find the moral gray area in what I was doing, which was exactly what I was looking for. But I also knew that she would be angry, if she was even capable of feeling any particular emotion. She didn't know that I knew about her making a move on Mason, which would make it easy for me to feign innocence when I told her we slept together. And, sure, I wanted to see the look on her face. Part of me reveled in it, just a little bit, because I finally had something that she actually *wanted*. A lot of girls at school might be jealous of me for dating Ben Carrera and having the social life, the grades, and the whole "Miss Perfect" thing, which was a label I used to shy away from before I finally just decided to embrace it. But Jayne didn't care about any of that stuff, and it wasn't an act. She just genuinely did not care. I could never quite fix my eyes on the horizon Jayne seemed to be looking at, but she sure as hell knew where the North Star was that she was following, even if she was following it alone.

But you know, it felt good. To finally have something that I knew my sister wanted. Something she couldn't have, no matter how far above it all she was . . . That was pretty damn great, if I'm being honest.

"You should get a second phone." That was the only thing Jayne said the night I told her about Mason, which was about two weeks before Trevor's party. We were sitting on the bed in her room, and she didn't even bother looking up from her phone.

"Um, I just told you I lost my virginity to the guy I'm cheating on my boyfriend with, and that's all you have to say? Jaynie, this is a big deal!"

She heaved a sigh and finally looked up. "I know it is, Dee. And you probably want me to either tell you that this is awesome or chastise you for doing it all behind Ben's back instead of just breaking up with him. But the only actual advice I can give you is that you should have a second phone. Because Ben *loves* to snoop through yours, and if he finds out about this, he will destroy you."

I wanted to respond with some kind of clever comeback, but I didn't have one. Because, of course, she was right. Ben wasn't a violent kind of guy, but he was a deeply mistrustful kind of guy, and he could fly into a rage in two seconds flat. I guess, underneath all his hair pomade and bravado, he was still the insecure kid I met on the playground when we were in grade school. Maybe Juliet had come to the same realization about Paris, no matter how perfect he'd seemed on the outside.

Insecurity can make people kind, or it can make them cruel. I preferred to ignore how cruel Ben could be when he felt like it, but I knew other people had seen it too. It's harder to pretend when someone else is watching the same play you are, and what you call romance, they call tragedy. Once Mason and I started spending more time together, it became more and more difficult to play along with the version of my life I'd built up so carefully in my head.

"Don't worry," Jayne said, misreading the look on my face as being the look of someone thinking about logistics. "I still have my old flip phone from middle school before Steven let us get smartphones." Jayne loves to call our parents by their first names. It annoys the heck out of me, but I guess it makes her feel cosmopolitan or something. Like our parents aren't our parents; they just happen to be two adult roommates we live with in a massive old house.

Before I could respond, she hopped off her bed and went into her closet, digging around in the top shelf. She emerged a minute later, holding a small silvery blue flip phone.

"And it even still works," she said triumphantly, powering it on.

I hated the fact that her response to my telling her I'd slept with the only guy she'd ever had a crush on was to offer me a phone to better communicate with him behind my boyfriend's back. But I didn't hate it enough not to take the phone.

The weird thing about that phone was that on the night of Trevor's party, it was the only one I had with me. The last thing Jayne asked me before Liz and I stepped out the door was whether or not I had my *phone*. She said it with an emphasis on the word, and I knew that what she really meant was whether or not I had the phone she'd given me. Our little secret. I knew that Mason was going to be at Trevor's that night—kind of a big deal for him, considering he wasn't really into that sort of thing—and that he had something important to talk to me about. So of course I had both of my phones.

But Ben asked to borrow my phone almost as soon as we got to Trevor's, with some lame excuse that made me realize he might be getting suspicious about my . . . extracurricular activities. In that moment, I was so grateful for the second phone; I handed him my regular phone with a shrug. But I never got it back from him after that.

Until, of course, it was slipped back into my pocket at the very last minute, full of calls and texts I never saw. Calls from Jayne telling me to come home, that my parents were heading back because my dad forgot his insulin.

The insulin . . . Liz had told me in my room when we were getting ready for the party that she'd seen Jayne take my dad's insulin out of his bag. And I hadn't believed her. I mean, why would Jayne do that? Liz was pretty quick to drop the subject when I told her she was obviously wrong, and I just wrote it off as one more move in the petty chess game Liz seemed to be playing with my sister. Maybe not . . .

And the old flip phone? Who knows where that is now? But I hope somebody found it somewhere. I'd like them to see what we had, me and Mason. What was between us in those text messages. Maybe someone might still figure out what really happened that night. It all seemed so normal, so typical, until it wasn't.

THE NIGHT OF THE PARTY

I WAS ANGRY at Jayne for ratting us out. She claimed that my mom already knew about the party—that she'd heard about it from someone else's mom at Whole Foods. But I also knew that Jayne loved nothing more than creating chaos for the fun of it, and I had a hunch that she decided to tell our mom just to throw a wrench in our plans. It might have even had more to do with ruining Liz's good time than mine. Jayne never quite forgave Liz for what happened between her and Ben, or at least that's the impression she gave, and I frequently had to remind her to just let it go. Generally, she didn't listen. The night of the party, I even saw her messing with the "Best Friends" necklace I got for Liz. Liz only took it off to shower, and I caught

Jayne fiddling with it after Liz took it off and headed into the bathroom. At the time, I didn't think much of it, but I realize now she did something to the clasp.

Because, sure enough, a little while after we got to Trevor's party, Liz realized her necklace was missing. She was totally freaked out about it, and I just promised her that we would find it later. I told her it was probably in the car or something, but more likely it was lost forever in the cornfield. In that moment, I knew Jayne had definitely done something to it. I just didn't know why; I thought it was part of her continued petty obsession about Liz being my best friend.

Now it all makes sense.

Jayne wins.

Anyway, in the end, it didn't matter that Jayne told our parents about the party. They were still heading up to Chautauqua, and for some reason, they were still willing to trust us that we wouldn't go out that night. Jayne had been going on about some mysterious college guy she had been seeing, and she was still happy to kick us out of the house so she could have a night with him.

That's what I can't figure out. Jayne had it made that night. No parents, a cute guy coming over, and her sister out of the house for the night. It didn't make any sense to me when I saw her walk through the door of Trevor's house. I was on the stairs, and she didn't see me at first. Liz immediately went to run interference and find out what she was doing there. She practically tackled Jayne the second she stepped inside. The two of them talked, and then Jayne went to go get a drink while Liz came back in my direction.

But I ducked away. I was a little drunk already, and I really did not want to listen to Liz complain about Jayne and whatever had caused her to show up at the party. Besides, I wanted to track down Mason *without* Ben realizing what I was up to. After a minute of scanning the crowd for me, Liz gave a shrug and headed out the back door, probably toward the bonfire that was already blazing outside.

"Hey, Dee." Jayne materialized at the bottom of the stairs out of nowhere. The place was a crush of people; I have no idea how she managed to weave her way through the crowd and make it over to me so quickly. She filled me in on why she was there and handed me one of the drinks she was holding. "One for the road," she said. "But not literally. You're drinking it here before we leave. And I've been trying to call you and text you for an hour to tell you about Mom and Dad coming home. Where is your phone?"

"Ugh, Ben has it." I didn't bother going into the details.

She gave me a look that said *I told you so.*

"Yeah, yeah. I know. You were right. Cute outfit, by the way." I noticed that she was dressed exactly the same way I was. It seemed weird to me, but it was also very much like

Jayne to pull something like that just to mess with people who didn't expect to see both of us at the same party.

"Thanks," she said, giving me a wink. "It looks better on me."

Raising her cup to mine, she clinked the plastic together. "Cheers, dear."

"Cheers."

I took a big gulp and scanned the room again for Mason.

"Looking for someone?" Jayne asked casually.

"You know I am, and you know who it is."

"Want me to help you find him?"

I looked at Jayne, trying to figure out whether or not she was being sincere. Honestly, though, it sounded like we were running out of time before we'd have to head back home, and Mason had told me repeatedly that he needed to talk to me tonight. It wasn't a conversation I was looking forward to, because something told me it would mostly be him insisting that it was time for me to finally dump Ben and go public with our relationship. It would be absolute social ruin for me, and I was not too keen on the idea of being banished to Siberia for the rest of my senior year.

And anyway, what was Mason going to do with his life, be an artist? Not to sound cold, but I didn't really feel like being the sole breadwinner, no matter how hot my husband turned out to be. The more real things got with Mason, the more appealing the white-picket-fence life that Ben and I had built up in our minds seemed. I felt like Mason and I were just spinning out into totally different realities. He thought the fun we were having together was actually going to be something serious, and I couldn't fathom what made him believe that. What, just because we'd slept together? It had been fantastic, sure, but I was considering it a dress rehearsal for the real thing. Mason seemed to be under the impression that it actually *was* the real thing.

In the end, Mason was the fling. Maybe Juliet should have ended up with Paris and saved herself all the trouble of Romeo. Long-term commitment over temporary passion, you know? That's obviously how my parents had built their marriage, and it seemed to be working pretty well for them so far. It's not like my mom even had to work.

"Yeah," I said finally. "Thanks. I've been texting him on the other phone; I just haven't heard back yet. He must be around here somewhere."

"I'll see if he's outside," Jayne said. "Meet me out there in ten minutes if I don't come back with him, okay? We really don't have all night."

Her phone pinged. She checked it and smiled to herself. "He's just too delicious," she said.

"Evan?" It wasn't even a guess. Jayne had a particular smile that always showed up when she and Evan were texting or talking with each other. Something about it always freaked me out a little bit, like there was some kind of big cosmic joke going on between the two of them that none of the rest of us knew about, and that joke was on us.

"He can't believe I'm actually here," she said. "He says barns are for horses. Not parties. I'll have to send him some Polaroids of all this. You know how he feels about proof."

That was the other weird thing—who actually sent Polaroid pictures to each other in the mail? God, my sister could be a weird one.

I rolled my eyes. "Give me a break. Now, are you going to help me find Mason or not?"

"Right, yeah. Meet me outside in a few. If I do find him, then at least we can make sure no one sees you guys together. I can be your lookout for Ben if he wanders by."

She glanced down at my Solo cup. "Drink up, Dee. You'll need some more liquid courage for whatever Mason has to say."

She wasn't wrong. Ugh, why had I let myself start something with him in the first place? I should have known it wouldn't be worth the hassle. I downed the rest of my drink.

"Remember to find me if I'm not back," Jayne said. "Who knows? I could wind up lost in a cornfield; you'll just discover my body when they mow this down for the Halloween maze."

I laughed. "I'll make sure you don't end up decomposing in a cornfield."

She held out her pinky. "Promise?"

I held mine out too. "Promise."

She disappeared, and I made my way down the stairs to check the living room. I could have sworn I saw Liz talking to Ben, but by the time I got to the place where they were, it seemed like the crowd of people had swallowed them up. I realized that I was starting to really feel the booze, and I vaguely wondered what the hell Trevor put in his so-called jungle juice. I stumbled for a minute and leaned against a wall for support.

"You good?" Some random guy appeared next to me. He seemed vaguely familiar—maybe we were in a class together?

"I'm good," I replied. Or, at least, that's what I thought I said. My mouth felt like it was filled with cotton. God, this was so embarrassing. How had I gotten this drunk? Vaguely, I felt a moment of relief that Ben wasn't around to see me like this. He always got so angry when I was wasted. Kind of funny, considering he was the one who got drunk and cheated on me. But now I had cheated on him. And, even better, I'd lost my virginity to someone else. Someone who wasn't him.

He would be so angry if he ever knew. I smiled to myself. I'd wait until the right moment in our marriage to bring that one out—what's that saying, revenge is a dish best served cold? It was becoming clear to me too that obviously that was how it would go. Mason was for fun, and Ben Carrera was for life. He was the future I should marry.

How much time had passed? It was weird; I was starting to feel like my arms weren't part of my body anymore. Like, I could see them moving as I made my way outside, but I couldn't feel them. When I got outside, I tried to take a few deep breaths to sober up. It didn't seem to be working too well, so I sat down and leaned against the outside of the house. Well, I didn't so much sit down as I slid down. My legs were starting to feel weird too. Something told me that this probably wasn't good, but I was tired, and I really couldn't be bothered to care.

"Sadie? Sadie! I've been looking for you everywhere." Mason's voice sounded like it was far away, but he was suddenly there, standing right next to me.

"Oh," I said. "Hey."

"Are you okay? God, you look hammered. How many drinks have you had?"

"Not that many," I tried to say. It didn't sound convincing.

"Can you stand up?"

I nodded, and Mason hoisted me up, putting my arm around his shoulder.

"God," he said. "Look, this really sucks. But there's something I need to show you, like, right now."

"Can't it wait?"

"I wish it could. And this isn't the thing I wanted to talk to you about, by the way—I swear to God, I had no idea about this. I just—I saw it, and I'm so glad I found you, because I didn't think you'd believe me if you didn't see it with your own eyes."

I had no idea what he was talking about, and all I wanted to do was close my eyes and go to sleep. But we were walking. My feet were moving. We were heading in the direction of the old stone barn. Did Mason want to hook up here, now? That was *not* happening.

Time seemed to stretch as we made our way toward the barn. It looked like it was a thousand miles away, floating in an ocean, and then suddenly we were at the door.

"Hey," Mason said, turning my face to his. I had a hard time focusing my eyes. "I'm sorry, Sadie. I hate to be the one to show you this, but like I said, you've gotta see it."

"What are you talking about?" My words sounded slurred to my own ears.

Mason let me go, and I swayed while he pulled open the barn door.

"Look," he whispered.

I did look. Or, at least, I tried to look. It was impossible to make sense of what I was seeing. Because I was standing in front of me and Ben, locked in the middle of an intense make-out session. But I was me, so how could I be there? I didn't understand it. My brain felt like it was covered in molasses. Nothing was working. I was *here.* I couldn't be there. Then, slowly, through the fog, it dawned on me.

It was Jayne. Jayne was with Ben. I stumbled into the barn and tried to say something, but I found myself sagging down onto the floor. Why couldn't I move my legs?

"What the hell?" Mason's voice sounded far away. So was the resounding thud of the barn door shutting, and suddenly Ben was on Mason, and Jayne was coming toward me.

This was not happening. Jayne was hooking up with Ben? No, impossible. I had just decided Ben was mine. Mason was fun; Ben was my future. Why was my twin stealing my future?

In the gaunt light of the bare bulb that illuminated the old barn, throwing shadows across the rusted-out tools and the rotting hay in the loft, I could see that my sister was holding something.

"I'm sorry, Dee," she said, not sounding sorry at all as she delivered the first blow. I knew it should have felt worse, but for some reason, I couldn't feel anything. The sound of her voice was at odds with the action she was taking. The violent way her arm was moving up and down. The warmth that seemed to be spreading all over my body.

Ben came into my field of vision, fuzzy and fading. I saw him take something out of his pocket and set it gently next to me. My phone. My real phone. Out of the corner of my eye, I could see Mason lying still on the floor. No one had to tell me he was gone, and no one needed to tell me that I was going too.

"Why?" I tried to ask, but the only sound that came out was a strange sort of wheeze.

"Here's the thing," Jayne said, standing up and tossing the knife to the floor. "I'm tired of being one of two. I'm one of one, Dee. And you were just . . . in the way. So was he"—she nods her head in the direction of Mason—"in the end. Too stupid to see what was standing right in front of him."

"You shouldn't have done it, Sadie." It was Ben's voice now, shaking and emotional. So very different from the voice of my sister. I knew then.

Jayne had told him everything about Mason. Ben had done it because he couldn't control his emotions.

So desperate for the love and approval of everyone. So desperate to be the best. The alpha. So desperate to be a leader.

Desperate enough for it that he would follow just about anyone.

"I'll catch you on the flip side, Dee," Jayne said as her voice and everything else began to fade. "Pinky promise."

The last thing I saw was the broken heart hanging around her neck. The one I went out and bought for her the day after Christmas, just because she couldn't stand someone else having something she didn't have.

The one Liz no longer had.

Jayne wins.

The last thing I heard was her perfectly architected scream.

The scream of a girl who had just found her sister murdered by the boy who was obsessed with her. The scream of a girl who was in shock and desperate for help. The sound of Ben yelling along with her, the grieving boyfriend who'd just discovered his girlfriend being murdered. Who did what he had to do and left the other guy dead too. I could very nearly hear them telling the police what happened. They would have a story. It would be perfect. No one would ever suspect them. Liz would be so heartbroken when she found out. The whole town would be, probably.

They would get away with it.

As everything faded, I could still hear the perfectly rehearsed scream of a girl who had just gotten away with murder.

JAYNE AND EVAN

SPRING BREAK, THE YEAR BEFORE

J: omg you would be DYING rn.

E: Tell me.

J: Tossed a little something "extra" in Liz's wine and she is SO messed up. My dad had to help her up the stairs and I might have then accused her of making a move on him.

E: Hahaha stop, that is tragic! More pls.

J: I mean not a bad start. Ur still coming for the weekend next month? Sensing a golden opportunity to up the stakes of the game.

E: I'm all ears xx

J: Two words: Liz and Ben.

E: YES. The game is on. Let's gooooooo!

ONE MONTH LATER

E: Last night got SO sloppy.

J: I'm literally right next to u. Texting, rly?

E: It's more fun with your whole fam at the table. Does S know yet?

J: Not yet, telling her as soon as you leave.

E: Staying on high alert waiting for THAT reaction. Do they even remember?

J: God, I'd be shocked. Idk tho, maybe Liz has built up a tolerance now that she's been roofied twice? Ben was so out of it, I doubt he remembers a thing.

E: Poor baby.

J: Ugh, no sympathy for him, pls.

E: I'm allowed to have sympathy for my fellow bro not being able to remember a hookup.

J: Gonna just go ahead and not acknowledge that. But you win for last night.

E: TY, love to have my work recognized. Keep him texting her too. Love that level of chaos for them.

J: U got it. But next one's mine. It's gonna be big.

E: Bar is high.

J: Don't worry, I'll reach it ;)

THE NIGHT OF THE PARTY

J: S and C just texted. On their way home now. S forgot his meds. That's my cue.

E: Wow, can't imagine how that happened . . . ;) Good work.

J: TY. Guess I HAVE to go to Trevor's now, can't even get ahold of Sadie to warn her . . .

E: Too bad. I know you wouldn't be caught dead at a party like that otherwise ;)

J: You know me so well.

AT THE PARTY

E: Oh my God. I'm dying. It's all true???

J: It's all true, babe.

E: Next time I'm in town, we're doing full-on barn party.

J: Only problem with that, I don't have a barn.

E: Whatever, barns are for horses anyway. But we'll commandeer one. What's next on the schedule? Game still on?

J: Still on.

E: Pics or it didn't happen ;) But only if ur sure. This is . . . BIG. No take-backs.

J: I know. Kinda in the mood for something permanent.

E: Ur insane. I don't hate it.

J: Idk about that. Just call me a little bit psychotic ;-)

E: Yes ma'am.

THE MORNING AFTER

E: U ok? Haven't heard anything. xx

J: Good, just got out of the station. Ben is w/ me. He was a good little helper.

E: OMG. U mean?

J: Game = Complete.

E: Holy shit. Bowing to the queen.

J: One of one now. True original.

E: That's my girl. U okay? Heavy shit.

J: Yeah. I'm ok. Free as a bird.

E: Free enough to start making plans for spring break? Senior year, baby :)

J: Grounded here for a hot minute, but gotta be all good by March. Count me in.

E: Yes! It's gonna be killer.

J: Cannot wait. x

ACKNOWLEDGMENTS

First and foremost, this book—and my writing career—would not be possible without my amazing and supportive husband, Ken. Thank you for being my brainstorming partner over countless late nights, our head chef while I was tucked away writing for months on end, and my biggest cheerleader. Our partnership is the engine powering every beautiful, crazy, marvelous risk I have felt bold enough to take. I also owe a note of appreciation to our four-legged family members, my favorite companions: Phryne the cat, who we still miss dearly, Olive the dog, and Hope the horse.

To my parents, who decided that encouraging their daughter to major in creative writing was a sensible thing to do (spoiler alert: it was). To my grandmother, who taught me that a house full of books and chocolate is one of the great secrets to happiness. And to my dear family—particularly my own brilliant sister and bonus sisters—and friends, whose unwavering support has kept my writing dreams going strong. Especially Joe and Amy—your belief has always come with a side of great food and wine, uncontrollable laughter, and a cozy place to stay. I owe you dinner in perpetuity.

I had an unreasonable amount of fun writing this book, and that is largely thanks to my phenomenal agent, Emily, and my fearless and brilliant editor, Kara. You both helped bring this story to life in such a delicious way. Thank you for everything! To my publicist Alex Kelleher-Nagorski, managing editor Art Morgan, jacket designer Heather Palisi, publisher Valerie Garfield, and the rest of the wonderful team at S&S: You have helped my biggest dreams come true in spectacular fashion. Thank you so much for your support!

Finally, I would not be writing today if not for the belief and inspiration of so many amazing English teachers and professors throughout my academic life. Thank you for taking me, and my ambitions, seriously. You made all the difference, and I am eternally grateful.

ABOUT THE AUTHOR

RACHEL PETERSON graduated from Miami University of Ohio with a degree in English and creative writing. Born and raised in Ohio, she started her career in advertising before spending nearly a decade in New York City as a marketing executive for technology companies. An avid traveler, Rachel now splits her time between Manhattan and the Midwest, where she lives with her husband, Ken; their dog, Olive; and her horse, Hope.